THE RESTLESS HEART

Isabella Oakley is travelling to her relations who are to sponsor her for the London season, when her aunt is taken ill en route. However, she meets the attractive Anthony Davenport, and his scheming sister Pamela, who take Bella to London in their private coach. Then Bella encounters the mysterious Mr Montcalm, whom Anthony warns her away from. Yet Montcalm seems to be following her . . . Will Bella and Anthony overcome the machinations of his relatives and find love?

Books by Kate Allan
in the Linford Romance Library:

FATEFUL DECEPTION

KATE ALLAN

THE RESTLESS HEART

Complete and Unabridged

LINFORD
Leicester

First published in Great Britain in 2006

First Linford Edition
published 2007

British Library CIP Data

Allan, Kate
    The restless heart.—Large print ed.—
Linford romance library
    1. Love stories
    2. Large type books
    I. Title
    823.9'2 [F]

    ISBN 978–1–84617–827–6

Published by
F. A. Thorpe (Publishing)
Anstey, Leicestershire

Set by Words & Graphics Ltd.
Anstey, Leicestershire
Printed and bound in Great Britain by
T. J. International Ltd., Padstow, Cornwall

1

'Anthony!' said the sharp female voice. 'Oh do go and help that poor creature out of her misery. I can hardly bear to watch.'

Isabella Oakley had two choices — turn around to observe the female who had spoken or plunge forward in one last-ditch attempt to save her bonnet from being blown completely away. She plunged forward, but a strong gust of wind got there first, lifting the straw bonnet with its frayed ribbons up into the air and farther across the lawn.

'Heavens!' she muttered, biting her lip and knowing that young ladies such as she were not supposed to look so utterly undignified. Bella put her hand up to the side of her head and felt hair coming loose. She'd now lost a hairpin as well. By now, all the people who had been enjoying a promenade on this pleasantly sunny afternoon in York would have stopped to watch the spectacle she was making of herself. They were most likely in better circumstances than she and could have let the elements take a bonnet with the certainty they could afford to buy a new one.

She shuddered to think how much her aunt and uncle had already spent on her wardrobe to make sure she would be properly outfitted for her debut in this spring of 1812.

Bella gripped her skirts in her hand and darted forward once more as the bonnet took off from the lawn and got caught in the branches of a tree above her.

She stood next to the tree trunk and looked up with some dismay. Maybe if she balanced on her tiptoes and reached up with her right hand . . . ?

'Miss,' a deep voice said. 'Allow me.'

A tall gentleman dressed wholly in black save his starched white linen cravat reached up into the branches of the tree and plucked out the bonnet.

'It appears beyond repair, I'm afraid,' he said, turning the squashed straw over in his long-fingered hands.

'Thank you, sir,' Bella looked up as he handed her the article and found herself looking into some very dark brown eyes squinting because of the sunlight. He had a long face with a square chin yet his strong features were softened by the tousles of his dark hair. Curls framed his forehead and around his ears, and rested in sharp contrast on his brilliant white neck cloth.

His gaze narrowed and Bella realised he was not simply trying to keep the sun out of his eyes but was regarding her with some curiosity. It was perhaps not surprising as her green serge dress was unfashionable. She looked down to the tops of his black leather boots and felt a heat rising in her cheeks.

'Anthony Davenport,' he said and gave a small bow as was customary. 'Your obedient.'

He kept one hand behind his back.

His manners were clearly those of high society. What was she supposed to do? She had no idea whether she should introduce herself or simply thank the stranger and be on her way. Her uncle was going to be cross enough as it was that she had gone out for a walk alone.

'Are you not going to share with me your name?' he said his voice as smooth as cream as he raked his hand through his hair. Yet she had the strangest sensation that he was a little nervous.

'Isabella Oakley.' Whether or not he was nervous she was — her cheeks were burning and she'd already forgotten his name. Anthony something . . . ?

'A pleasant day for taking a turn, Miss Oakley,' he went on to say, a small smile pulling at the corners of his mouth.

Bella's attention turned to the conversation of two fast-approaching ladies.

'What a circus,' one of the ladies said.

Bella wanted to hide her head in her hands. She should have noticed one of the ribbons on her bonnet was fraying and then none of this would have happened. But she'd been in such a thoughtless rush as usual . . .

The second lady said, 'Well, Anthony is busy making an acquaintance. One day he really will disgrace us all!'

The conversation ended there as Bella turned to look at the ladies, now only a few yards away and approaching purposefully with formidable-looking smiles.

'Anthony,' the lady who had last spoken said. Her puce-coloured dress gave a final swish against her ankles as she and her companion drew to a halt.

'Miss Oakley,' he said with the briefest of nods, 'may I present my sister, Miss Pamela Davenport, and our friend, Miss Georgina Shuttleworth.'

The two ladies nodded but neither showed a hint of deference. The sister wore a haughty expression and a fashionably-straight cut black Spencer jacket over her walking dress although a jaunty ostrich feather graced her black felt hat.

The friend looked far less military, but equally luxurious in an apple green silk gown covered by a grey and probably sable-trimmed pelisse.

Bella smiled and tried to stop herself blinking too rapidly.

'Miss Oakley,' said the sister, tapping her fingers on the handle of her pink parasol, 'are you here in York on business or for pleasure?'

'I am travelling with my aunt and uncle to London so I am afraid our stay in York is very brief.'

'Oh?' A perfectly-curved eyebrow was raised. 'What a pity we will not have time to make your acquaintance, Miss Oakley. We hope you enjoy your stay in York and have a pleasant and safe journey on to London.'

'Good day.' Bella swallowed and nearly tripped backwards in her haste to be gone from the awkward situation. She wasn't even sure if the sister had snubbed her or not! How was she going to survive in London when her knowledge of manners and etiquette, and people, was so small?

The straw from her crushed bonnet pushed into the palm of her hand painfully and she quickened her pace without looking back. She would survive. Somehow. There was always a way.

She went through the avenue of the New Walk and back into the city and to *The Swan*.

Bella arrived there with not a minute to spare before Uncle Samuel returned. How cross he would be if he knew not only what had happened to her best Dunstable straw bonnet, but also that she had disobeyed him by leaving the inn at all. She stood quietly in the room they had secured as a private parlour as he removed his woollen great coat.

'Bella, what has happened to your bonnet? Have you been abroad?' Her uncle stroked his greying whiskers.

'I took a short walk to . . . '

'Fie, no time for that now, tell me later.' He looked about in a distracted fashion. 'Go and pack up your things.

An old friend of mine, Charles Sinclair has kindly invited us to stay at their house.'

Who were they, the Sinclairs? Bella wanted to ask, but she held her counsel. Uncle Samuel wore a worried frown.

'It will be much better for your aunt,' he muttered, 'though *The Swan* is comfortable enough, granted.'

Bella went straight upstairs. Folding her clothes was no chore, she had never had her own maid, and she was quickly packed and ready.

The Sinclairs lived in a fashionable part of the city called Bootham in a tall, well-proportioned house painted the colour of grey stone. They sent their own carriage to the inn as her uncle and aunt did not possess their own private conveyance. Charles Sinclair was also an attorney, like her uncle Samuel, but clearly one with a superior income.

His wife, Jane, was in a flattering mauve day dress which complemented her dark hair and immediately began to fuss about Aunt Harriet no sooner had they stepped inside.

Bella watched Mr Sinclair clap Uncle Samuel on the back and lead him off into the depths of the house and then found herself ushered into the drawing room, papered in lemon yellow and furnished with fashionable delicate rosewood pieces.

The day did not necessitate a fire and Bella perched on one of the sofas and let the sunshine coming through the windows warm her back.

She wasn't alone for long. Mrs Sinclair swept in and sat down beside her. 'How delightful to have visitors,' she said, arranging her skirts. 'York has quite the finest Assembly Rooms in the North, far better than Harrogate or Newcastle, and a better quality of people than anywhere outside London, except, grant you, Brighton or Bath. Really, there is hardly a need to go to London we have so many people of fashion who come here.'

'I think . . . ' Bella began. She wanted

to explain how very important it was to her aunt that she did her London season. Aunt Harriet had been talking about it for years.

There was a tap on the door, and Bella sank back into the chair as a maid brought in tea on a large white tray. A footman rushed ahead and pulled one of the rosewood tables into place and the maid set down her tray before they both nodded and left the room.

Mrs Sinclair's attention snapped back to Bella. 'I thought you might be parched,' Mrs Sinclair said. 'Now my dear, what have you seen of the city?'

'This morning I went to the New Walk. It was very nice and there were some people of fashion, ladies mostly.' And a rather tall, handsome gentleman immaculately dressed who had been rather charming and gallant. And she'd made a fool of herself, but she was not going to mention any of that to Mrs Sinclair.

'How pleasant,' Mrs Sinclair lifted her teacup. 'Did your aunt have some benefit from the fresh air?'

'Oh, no. I was there . . . alone.'

Mrs Sinclair spluttered and coughed. She set her cup down with a rattle. 'You mean to say you were out quite alone?'

Bella nodded. She often went out alone in Hexham, but it did not seem like a time to mention this fact.

'Oh dear, oh dear. My child this will never do!' Mrs Sinclair dabbed her mouth with her napkin. 'Now, have you been to the Assembly Rooms?'

'No — '

'Ah! Well, we shall go then. This evening.'

'This evening, Mrs Sinclair?'

'Certainly, for if we don't go tonight we shall have to wait until Thursday for the next ball and your aunt will be most likely fully recovered by then and you half the way to London.'

Bella did not think so. When Aunt Harriet was struck with her nervous complaint she suffered severe headaches, and then was left for days after fatigued

11

and with spirits much depressed.

Bella shivered. The heat hit her as she walked with Mr and Mrs Sinclair and her uncle into the Grand Assembly Room later that night.

She recalled Aunt Harriet's soft-spoken words. 'A husband does not find a wife on the basis of her proficiency at the pianoforte. You have good deport-ment, demeanour and can dance well, and you have twenty thousand pounds besides.'

Mr and Mrs Sinclair had the acquaintance of many people and Bella found herself being introduced to group after group. Already her fingers were damp in her satin gloves and her mind spun as she tried to remember all the names and faces.

'Look at the gentleman over there,' Mrs Sinclair's voice was so low Bella had to strain to hear it.

She looked — and found herself looking at the gentleman who had rescued her bonnet! He was talking to some ladies so that she saw his sharp profile with his long nose and firm jaw. He rested one fist, as was polite, behind his back.

'That is Mr Anthony Davenport,' Mrs Sinclair said. 'See how he is standing with one leg a step in front of the other and slightly bent at the knee? Well, think of a Davenport bureau. Have you seen one? I find them a bit masculine. I prefer a French escritoire to use for writing correspondence. Think of a Davenport nonetheless, crafted with a curved leg.'

Mrs Sinclair touched her elbow. 'Ah, Miss Davenport!'

Miss Davenport arrived in front of them looking splendidly modish in a buttermilk muslin which set off her auburn hair that was pinned into curls. 'Good evening, Mrs Sinclair. Miss Oakley, isn't it?'

'Y-yes,' Bella managed. Why did her own hair have to be so very dull, brown and ordinary? 'Good evening.'

'You are already acquainted?' Mrs Sinclair enquired.

'We met briefly. Earlier today.' Miss Davenport pushed her chin in the air.

'Miss Oakley is our guest,' Mrs Sinclair said with a frown. 'Along with her uncle and aunt.'

Miss Davenport raised her eyebrows. 'How lovely.'

Bella regarded the floor. It was so much more pleasant to look at Miss Davenport's silk dancing slippers than her critical gaze.

A male voice broke in. 'Miss Oakley?'

Bella lifted her chin and found herself looking into the brown eyes of Mr Anthony Davenport. He bowed stiffly.

She suddenly realised his sister was speaking, saying something inconsequential to Mrs Sinclair. Before she had time to pick up what had been said Mr Davenport had taken a step towards her and felt so close that she was sure she could feel his breath on her cheek.

'Would you do me the honour . . . '

2

'Would you do me the honour of this dance?' Bella froze at Mr Davenport's deep timbre, but his eyes did not catch hers and his arm was held out not towards her but to Mrs Sinclair.

Mrs Sinclair smiled as she took it and Bella fought against the feeling of pique and disappointment. Whatever it was, it had made her chest feel tight and her heart beat a little too quickly. She really must be vain to think that a dashing gentleman such as Mr Davenport would ask her to dance.

Her eyes followed their progress and she found it hard to stop herself thinking what a fine figure Mr Davenport cut.

Her uncle and Mr Sinclair took the opportunity to retreat to the card room, leaving her in the company of Miss Davenport. Bella struggled to think of something to say.

'It is a surprise to see you here, Miss Oakley. I had no idea that you were staying with Mrs Sinclair. Are you in York for long?'

'I . . . I am not sure. We are bound for London, but my aunt is rather poorly.'

'I hope your aunt will be better soon. There really is nothing worse than to be taken ill while travelling, which is fatiguing in any case. We are bound for London tomorrow. We have a house there.'

'Really?' Bella said. 'Is it anywhere near Brook Street?'

'Yes, it is indeed on Brook Street. How clever of you to mention Brook Street of all places!' Miss Davenport opened her white fan and fanned herself lightly. 'It is, as I am sure you must have read, a most superior street.'

'I am going to stay with my aunt and uncle in London. Their house is on Brook Street.'

'Oh?' Miss Davenport stepped back a

pace, as if she had almost lost her balance. 'Are you sure?'

'Yes,' Bella said. 'In Brook Street in the West End.'

'Then I must have your cousin's acquaintance?' Miss Davenport patted Bella lightly on the arm.

'The Honourable Mr and Mrs Charles Cavenham. Mrs Cavenham was my father's sister. Do you know of them?'

'Know of them!' Miss Davenport's countenance was wreathed in smiles. 'The Cavenhams are a very well regarded family and they go everywhere. You will have a splendid time! Now we surely will see each other in London and if you have a spare moment you must come and call.'

Bella felt herself relax a little and she ventured a smile. 'Thank you very much, Miss Davenport.'

'Oh, do call me Pamela! Knowing Clarissa Cavenham you will be engaged to some duke by then . . . ' Miss Davenport looked at her empty glass and then Bella's. 'Would you like some more punch?'

'Oh, I shouldn't.' Bella shook her head but Pamela called to a young man who happened to be passing.

'Henry! Do be a dear!' Henry shortly returned with two brand new glasses of punch.

'Thank you, Henry. This is Miss Isabella Oakley. Miss Oakley, Mr Henry Bolling.'

He was a reed-thin man with a lop-sided smile. He winced and blinked with a single eye as one of the violins erred slightly out of tune. 'Miss Oakley, would you do me the honour — '

'Next dance, Bolling,' came the clipped, assured tones of Mr Davenport.

The contrast was startling. Mr Davenport stood tall and still while Mr Bolling bowed and stepped back.'

Bella's heart felt as if it was beating in her throat. It seemed as though his vital presence filled all the space around them. She gingerly reached forward to touch his solid sleeve. 'Thank you, that would be delightful.'

She decided she must have too active an imagination encouraged by too much punch and she did not fully appreciate how, of all the men in the room, Mr Davenport was the only one who seemed to stand out to her.

He swept her forward where couples were making up sets for the next dance.

She concentrated on trying to forget she was dancing with a handsome man, and pretended instead it was her dancing master.

She hoped that she acquitted herself to his satisfaction, but he said nothing after the dance ended except the usual pleasantries.

She could hardly believe he had wanted to dance with her, but it must have been simply politeness. Her chest felt weak. Crushed. 'Thank you, Mr Davenport,' she said.

'Now where is your uncle, or Mrs Sinclair?' he said, looking about the ballroom and not for a moment at her.

'For I would deliver you back to them.'

There was a loud cough behind them, and a blond-haired gentleman with an eager smile came forward and begged an introduction. Bella found herself whisked into the next set.

He seemed a nice enough young man, but his dancing was not up to that of Mr Davenport's. It took all her concentration to dance properly and not end up tripping.

After the dance her partner fetched her a glass of lemonade. She looked about, but could not see Mrs Sinclair or the Davenports anywhere. Should she go into the card room to her uncle?

Pamela Davenport's voice cut through the air like glass, coming from behind her. 'Anthony, listen! Why do you not go and find Miss Oakley and dance with her again?'

Bella turned her head to see Miss Davenport and her friend standing on the other side of the column. They had not noticed her.

Mr Davenport's reply came in an

even, measured voice that betrayed no emotion. 'I already danced with Miss Oakley. I have no plans to waste her time and mine and raise false expectations by asking her to dance again.'

'Miss Oakley is quite a delightful girl and pretty,' Miss Davenport snapped. 'Do go and dance with her again!'

Mr Davenport gave an uneasy laugh. 'What has Miss Oakley done to so absolutely recommend herself to you, my dear sister?'

'Her aunt is the Honourable Clarissa Cavenham.'

'Not all of us are so mercenary,' Mr Davenport replied in a stiff voice. He turned on his heel and walked away in the direction of the card room.

Bella gulped and stayed motionless behind the pillar. She saw that her hand was trembling as she raised her glass of lemonade to her lips and took a large sip.

'Isabella! There you are.' Miss Sinclair was advancing towards her and came up to her side.

'It appears your connection with the Cavenhams has come out. I have heard several people remark upon it.' Miss Sinclair continued to speak behind her fan. 'You do realise your relatives are of the haute monde?'

Bella ventured a smile. The idea that everyone was talking about her was horrifying. She should never have mentioned the Cavenhams to Pamela Davenport.

'And your dance with Mr Anthony Davenport has certainly set you up. Any young lady he dances with is immediately singled out by the rest of the young gentlemen keen to get in on what he has spotted.'

'He has a . . . reputation?' Bella gasped.

'A reputation as a most eligible young man who is most careful who he dances with,' Mrs Sinclair replied with a frown. 'And now his elder brother is dead, he is most sought after . . . '

She broke off at the approach of another gentleman and whispered,

'Bella, this young man has ten thousand a year and a coach and four, I do believe.'

To the gentleman who was dressed in a dark green frock coat and with hair that looked like a pat of muddied straw, she said, 'Mr Montcalm, what a pleasure.'

Bella found herself thinking he was dressed rather shabbily for someone with ten thousand a year, but she smiled politely nonetheless and resigned herself to another dance.

She was swiftly removed from Mr Montcalm's presence as their dance ended by a firm hand at her elbow. Mr Davenport's countenance was dark as thunder. What had tickled him so?

There was something about his determined presence that made her happy to comply as he pushed them into a quiet corner.

Bella flicked open her fan and looked directly into his strong eyes. Being propelled across the ballroom against her will was intolerable! Had he something of import to say to her, he should surely have merely requested her company?

She raised her voice. 'Mr Davenport, what is the meaning — '

'Mr Montcalm, although charming of manner, is not a suitable gentleman for you to strike up an acquaintance.'

Mrs Sinclair had said nothing about Mr Montcalm being unsuitable. In fact, quite the opposite. Bella thrust her chin a little higher and stared defiantly into Mr Davenport's dark eyes. She was pleased to see he flinched slightly, but quickly regained his composure.

She said, 'How so?'

Mr Davenport's lips thinned. 'You will be satisfied with my word on the matter.'

'I am told he has ten thousand a year.'

Mr Davenport frowned. 'If you will marry a man for that, it is a pity.'

It was as if the room had suddenly emptied and there was no longer music, dancing and chatter but only a gentleman who was looking at her in a manner she was sure no gentleman ever had done. Her skin prickled for some reason she could not fathom.

He looked away and pulled at his cravat. 'I think, even if you dislike me, Miss Oakley, we should try to do our best to rub along as we shall be much in each other's company until we reach London.'

'How is this to be?'

'It has been arranged for you to join us to travel down to London. We leave tomorrow.'

'You may be leaving tomorrow, Mr Davenport, but I decline the invitation.'

'I'm afraid you have no choice in the matter. My sister is most eager to gain a travelling companion. It has all been arranged.'

'How — '

'Miss Oakley,' he said, his voice laced with warning. 'I understand that your uncle, anxious about your aunt's health, is to return home as soon as possible and therefore, if you wish to get to

London without causing a great deal of difficulty, I propose you reconsider.'

Mr Davenport — '

'I have sworn to your uncle that I shall be responsible for your safe arrival, and I shall. You need have no concern that you are travelling with strangers. We are acquaintances of long standing of both Mr and Mrs Sinclair and of the Honourable Mr and Mrs Cavenham.'

A rosy-cheeked young man not a day older than Bella herself had arrived at her side, a hopeful look set on his face. He asked Bella to dance and Mr Davenport turned on his heels, his jaw looking as if it was set in stone.

Bella allowed herself to be led away, and forced her breathing to be steady. She was excited by the prospect of the journey to London despite Mr Davenport's high-handed manner and his sister's fickle change of opinion after she had discovered that Bella was a person of consequence.

Bella woke. Where was she? She

stared up at the elegant, white plaster ceiling high above her for a moment before remembering. She was in York at the house of Mr and Mrs Sinclair.

Today she joined the Davenports to journey to London. Their coach was coming at ten o'clock.

Bella yawned. She had been so excited she had not gone to sleep until very late. She glanced at the small clock on the mantelpiece. Nearly nine! She rushed out of bed, struggling out of the heavy counterpane, splashed water from the ewer into the pretty wash-basin, and then changed her mind twice about what to wear.

She would settle on her rather plain, but well-cut violet and cream pinstriped day dress.

Ten o'clock came round all too quickly. Bella kissed her aunt, uncle and the Sinclairs goodbye, only to have them all stand around for several minutes as some of the luggage had to be unpacked to make room for her trunk.

'Ready to go now!' Mr Davenport said at last, offering her his hand to help her up into the coach.

It was a handsome conveyance, well-sprung and painted burgundy red with the monogram GD, which she assumed must be that of a more senior Davenport, emblazoned on each side.

There was space for four inside the coach and the fourth was Pamela's maid, Alice. Their party was completed by two outriders.

With the finely furnished cream silk and dark green velvet interior, Bella was sure she was not used to such luxury. But she did want the Davenports to think her provincial.

She copied Pamela who was silent and stared out of the window as they queued in the traffic of the city and then gathered speed as they travelled through the village of Fulford and out into open countryside.

'When shall we stop for luncheon?' Pamela asked her brother who, quite properly, sat beside her.

Bella could not help letting her gaze trail to his heavily cut coat of forget-me-not blue and then his doe skin breeches which fitted so perfectly without a crease. His butterscotch cravat was starched and it seemed to serve to hold up his clean-shaven chin.

'Not until we are past Selby,' he replied.

'How far is that?' Pamela pouted.

'An hour, no more.'

There was no further conversation after that, but the coach was comfortable and the scenery interesting enough, albeit flat.

'Miss Oakley?' a low voice was saying.

'Oh! Oh, dear!' She must have fallen asleep! Bella felt her cheeks go red and she righted herself. Was it lunchtime already? The coach had stopped and they were in a town.

'The coachman is paying the toll for the bridge,' Mr Davenport said and smiled. The way he looked at her made her want to blush all the more. 'We are in Selby.'

Bella stared out of the window where the breeze coming in was thankfully cool. The horses jolted and walked over the magnificent drawbridge over the river which was bursting with ships and packet boats.

They did not stop for lunch until some way past Selby, at a coaching inn called The George in a village Bella missed the name of.

She followed Pamela into a private sitting room and copied her as she sat down and held her hands still on her lap and chin high as if arranged for a portrait.

Several minutes ticked past and a maid brought them tea.

'Where on earth is my brother?' Pamela said. 'Miss Oakley, I must apologise for my brother's behaviour. He has quite forgotten himself.'

'Please do not worry on my account,' Bella replied.

'Of course,' Pamela added, 'he really is not a bad brother at all, quite the opposite. Any girl would be fortunate to be his sister.'

'Indeed.' Bella smiled and wondered whether there was something more enlightening she ought to have said. But she had not brothers or sisters herself which she could comment on.

Pamela leaned forward a little. Her voice came very low. 'Our dear father has been ill these past two years and Anthony has had to take on most of the responsibilities of head of the family. But he does wear it well.'

'Is anyone to marry him?' Bella found herself asking and then wished she had a fan in her hands she could open to distract herself from her impertinence.

'He is quite unattached — '

Rat-a-tat! The door burst open. 'I am sorry, I was delayed,' Mr Davenport said and tugged at his cravat with a frown. 'Have you enjoyed the journey so far, Miss Oakley?'

'Yes, thank you. It has been very comfortable.'

Bella watched him flick his forget-me-not coat tails back to take a seat, and thought how he managed to be masterful and yet elegant at the same time.

There was something about his presence in the room that demanded everyone's attention. Pamela had said how handsome, eligible and of good character her brother was and she was right.

They enjoyed the light repast and were shortly on the road again.

It was overcast, but it had been a pleasant day, fairly warm and with no rain. Bella distracted herself from her thoughts by concentrating on looking out of the window for a while and watched the fields and pastures go by. Pamela and Mr Davenport were talking about some people they knew, but of whom she had never heard.

Suddenly Pamela clutched her hands about her waist. Pain flashed across her countenance. She cried out. 'Oh, Alice, I do feel quite unwell!'

'What is it?' Alice asked, leaning forward.

'Perchance it is something I have eaten!'

'Perhaps that mutton we had at luncheon was a bit old?' Mr Davenport said as if he was talking about the weather. 'Or that pickle? Miss Oakley, did you eat any of the pickle?'

'No,' Bella replied. Why was Mr Davenport unperturbed by his sister's sudden indisposition?

'I did!' Pamela said, doubling forward. 'Oh, dear, I do think I may be sick!'

3

Pamela tumbled out of the coach and ran behind some nearby bushes with Alice at her heels.

Bella jumped down, holding on to the door. The ground was wet.

'What's going on?' came Mr Davenport's voice behind her. 'Wait there! I'll give you a hand.'

'Your sister is ill,' Bella replied without looking back over her shoulder. 'It must have been the pickle at the inn.'

A firm hand gripped her shoulder. 'I will see what is happening.'

'What is happening is that your sister is being sick!' Bella swung around to face him so he was forced to let go of her. 'I doubt she will welcome interference from a gentleman. Even her brother!' His brow looked so furrowed she quickly added, 'I will go and see what is happening.'

What was happening was that Pamela had just finished being violently sick and was being helped by Alice to regain her composure. Bella returned to the coach where Mr Davenport stood stroking the mane of one of their chestnut horses.

He looked pale. At least he had some concern now for his sister, Bella noted with satisfaction and told him the news.

'We had better stop at the next inn,' he said to the coachman.

'Aye, thar's *The Four Alls* five miles hence,' the coachman replied.

'Your sister will be fine,' Bella ventured.

Mr Davenport turned and stared at her with a dark look, but did not speak. She watched his hand ball into a fist before he seemed to have to force it to ease itself.

Bella hastened to help Pamela who was making her way slowly back to the coach. She looked quite green. How lucky she herself had not touched any of that pickle!

The coach proceeded slowly, but it was hardly above half-an-hour before they reached an inn where Mr Davenport declared they were to stay for the night and immediately set about sending for a doctor and to see that his sister was put in the best room and had every comfort.

What with all this going on around her, Bella decided it would be best to slip out of the way. She found a sitting-room at the very front of the inn where she sat alone and quite undisturbed and watched the doctor arrive.

A good deal of time passed and Bella realised she was hungry. Had the doctor departed yet? She looked out of the window. As soon as he left she would trouble someone for a sandwich.

She would not have credited that an inn could be so busy even as night was falling. Three men were busy unloading sacks from a cart into the malthouse. Then a dangerous-looking curricle was skilfully brought to a halt by its young gentleman driver. He had a young lady at his side who looked quite pale and nearly tripped as he helped her down.

Was this a romantic elopement? Two elderly ladies arrived in a coach nearly as grand as the Davenports'. They conversed with the young couple and were obviously of the same party. It was not an elopement after all!

Bella watched as they rode on again shortly without coming into the inn. It must be full, Bella considered looking at the fire that was burning low. Should she trouble to ask for a servant.

A flash of tan and a black horse in the corner of her eye drew her gaze back to outside.

A man in a tan-coloured great coat had just arrived and dismounted. He handed the reins of his horse to the ostler. He turned around and she recognised him at once — Mr Montcalm from York Assembly Rooms!

Bella jumped at the sound of knocking on the door. 'Come in.'

It was Alice.

'How is Miss Davenport?' Bella

asked, now unable to see out of the window as Alice came to stand in front of it.

'I think she is feeling a little better. The doctor has been, miss.'

'Yes, I saw.'

Alice lowered her eyelids and said, 'Miss, Mr Davenport asks that you join him for dinner. He is in the private dining-room waiting.'

Mr Davenport had requested her company at dinner! Bella looked down at her pin-striped dress in dismay. There was no time to change if he was already waiting for her. She glanced back out into the yard, but of Mr Montcalm or his mount there was no sign. Had he come into the inn? Or ridden on?

She needed to find her chamber first and then meet Mr Davenport for dinner. Whether or not Mr Montcalm was at this inn should mean nothing to her. But her curiosity was piqued — most especially because Mr Davenport had been so resolute in warning her against that gentleman.

Bella left the sitting-room and came into the hallway where she asked one of the servant girls to show her to her chamber.

It was a small but clean and pleasant enough room, but with no looking glass! She took out her comb and adjusted her hair the best she could and decided that it would be foolish to try and change now with not a gown yet unpacked from her portmanteau and that she would have to make the best of it in her pin stripe.

She ventured back downstairs and knocked at the door of the room next to the sitting-room she had been in and heard a deep male voice say, 'Come in!'

He was alone in the room and stood with his back to the door and her and did not turn around, but said, 'Miss Oakley, please sit down.'

She obeyed. There were two places laid at the table, one at the head and one just beside. Pamela must have a tray upstairs — if she was eating at all.

'Is Miss Davenport feeling any better?' Bella asked.

'A little.' His eyes narrowed and he seemed to deliberately soften his expression back to the urbane disinterest of before. 'Thank you for your concern.'

He moved to the table and pulled her chair out for her. 'Miss Oakley, it appears that my sister's indisposition may necessitate a slight delay to our journey. I hope this will not inconvenience you too much. I would be happy to make some alternative arrangements for your onward journey to London if you are unhappy to be delayed?'

'I am not unhappy — '

Bella jumped back at the sound of a pistol shot.

'What!' Mr Davenport was at the door before she could think what was going on. 'Stay here!' He disappeared, slamming the door behind him.

A pistol shot? Bella clutched the back of the chair and took several deep breaths. Was there a robbery going on?

She darted to the window and hid behind the curtain.

Out in the yard all seemed quiet. Too quiet.

And then the ostler, with arms flapping, appeared from the direction of the stables with Mr Davenport, mounted on a splendid black stallion. The ostler patted the animal's rump, and with a skittish kicking of his heels, he was off carrying Mr Davenport out of the yard and on to the road at a canter.

Bella ran out of the dining-room and found her way outside to the inn yard.

'Miss?' The ostler looked at her with surprise.

'What's happening?' Bella demanded. She struggled for breath. 'Where has Mr Davenport gone?'

'A spot o' business,' the man replied and picked up a large horse-hair broom that had been resting by some barrels. He started to sweep. 'You had best be staying inside. It's gettin' dark, miss. He'll be back anon, I'll warrant ye.'

'But where has he gone? Did he not say?'

'Thar's nowt ye can do, miss. He went chasing that gentleman was 'ere earlier.'

'In the tan coat?' It had to be something to do with Mr Montcalm. She just knew it. Bella wrapped her arms about her and hugged herself. It was cold.

The ostler shook his head. 'His coat were black.'

'Are you sure?'

'Aye. The tan coated gentleman, he'd be inside, miss.'

'Th-thank you.' Bella stumbled back inside and shut the heavy wooden door behind her. What was going on?

She picked up her skirts and ran upstairs, nearly colliding on the landing with a maid carrying a tray.

'Watch out, miss!' The maid skilfully kept the tray from falling.

'I'm sorry.' Bella pressed her back against the wall so the maid could pass easily. 'Where is Miss Davenport's room?'

'Down there.' The maid nodded behind her. 'Last door on t'right.'

The door was shut fast. Bella turned the handle carefully, unsure whether it was wise to disturb Pamela at this hour, or whether she was being fanciful. Should she rather try and find Mr Montcalm, who most likely was enjoying supper downstairs, and satisfy herself that nothing in that quarter was amiss?

She pushed the door open steadily, and ventured into the dark, silent room. On the bed Pamela was sleeping. Had the doctor given her laudanum? Surely the room was too cold?

The curtains billowed. The sash window had been left ajar.

Bella approached the bed. If Pamela was only lightly sleeping she would wake her.

'Pamela?' Bella whispered. There was no answer.

She could not discern the rise and fall of Pamela's chest, or even hear breathing. A wave of panic came over

Bella and she reached out and touched Pamela's shoulder.

It was a pillow. The bed was stuffed with bolsters! Where was Pamela?

Bella ran to the window, a sudden painful feeling making her ribs feel as though they were being stuffed into too tight stays. She pulled the window wide open and gasped in the icy air.

The yard at the back of the inn was piled with boxes and crates. There was a large piece of lawn, and in its middle a hen house. To the right was a small orchard with a low stone wall. Then she saw movement. Someone was skirting along the side of the edge of the orchard, in the shadows, and trying to use the low wall for cover.

It looked like a woman.

Bella raced out of the chamber and downstairs. Now, how could she get out the back? From the kitchens of course!

The kitchen was sweltering with heat and steam from its huge range, and open spit fire.

'Miss?' The cook called after her.

'It's Miss Davenport! Help!' Bella managed and headed straight for the back door. It was locked.

She turned around to see the two kitchen maids and boot boy gaping at her.

'Help!' Bella felt foolish but what if Pamela was touched by the moon? Or something the doctor had given her was causing a temporary madness? 'She's outside. It's very cold outside.'

The cook, a matronly lady, waddled up and brought out a stout iron ring which held a dozen keys. 'Thar's the one.' Her chubby fingers slotted the right key in the door.

Or was Pamela trying to run away? Deliberately?

Bella sped outside with the kitchen maids and boot boy following. Through the yard and across the lawn and into the darkness and towards the orchard — black trees against a dark grey sky.

'Pamela?' Bella shouted. The woman must be Pamela. She stopped at the stone wall. The silence hung heavily in the air as the others came to a halt a pace behind her.

'Pamela? It's me, Isabella. Bella.'

A crunch of twigs sounded from the far side of the orchard, which Bella had seen from the window led on fields.

'Miss!' The kitchen boy pointed. A figure was moving rapidly towards them, her cloak half undone and flapping in a tangle about her legs.

Bella sat on the low wall and swung her legs up on to it, and then down the other side. She heard the ripping of material and knew she had somehow torn her dress. She jumped down on to her feet. The figure almost collided into her.

'Pamela?' Bella clutched her shoulders.

'Bella, I think we had better go back in,' Pamela said in a small voice which was very unsteady, as if she had been crying.

'What's going on? Pamela, are you all right?'

'Just a little cold,' Pamela said, not

answering her first question.

With help, they climbed back over the wall.

'Bella, will you please not say anything to Anthony, to my brother?' Pamela drew her cloak more tightly about her as they walked slowly across the lawn and back toward the inn.

Bella was unsure what to say, but of course she could not break a confidence, if asked. 'No, I will not.' She lowered her voice and whispered in Pamela's ear. 'But there are the servants?'

'There's a shilling each if you'll not say anything of this?' Pamela said in a voice that sounded more like herself.

The boot boy's eyes shone in particular.

'And for the cook,' Bella added. 'Let's go back via the kitchens.'

'We won't say owt, miss,' said one of the kitchen girls pushing a lock of hair from her face. 'Nor Cook neither.'

They got Pamela upstairs and into bed wrapped stoutly in flannels with very little fuss. Bella saw that the window was shut stoutly, and when she found a small bottle of laudanum on the dresser took the liberty of measuring a few drops into a honey tincture one of the maids had prepared.

'Drink this while it is hot — to warm you,' Bella said and came over to the bedside with it. 'There is laudanum, but the honey will disguise the bitterness.'

Pamela took the cup in both hands. 'Do not look at me like that! I cannot tell you what I was about.'

'I did not ask you to tell me,' Bella protested.

Pamela drank slowly and then sank back into the pillows. 'I will tell you when we are in London, not before. And you must keep to your promise of not telling my brother.'

Bella took the empty cup and nearly tripped. She had ripped her dress at the hem. She would change as soon as Pamela was sleeping. She tidied the bits and pieces back on to the tray. Gentle snores drifted across the room.

Bella decided. She would return the

tray to the kitchen, where she was sure Cook would find her something to eat. Her stomach rumbled with hunger.

Besides, she wanted to go back downstairs and see if there were any sign of Mr Davenport — or Mr Montcalm.

Balancing the tray on one hand, she shut Pamela's door carefully behind her.

'What are you doing?' came the thunderous tones of Mr Davenport. He stood on the landing, his chest heaving up and down with exertion — or anger. He was still wearing his riding gloves and had not changed his boots.

'Shhhhh!' Bella lifted a finger to her mouth. How dare he shout at her when she had just rescued his sister from . . . from goodness knows what! 'Pamela is sleeping.'

'She is?' His eyes darted about the corridor uneasily before he rounded on her again. 'Why are you carrying a tray? Where is the maid?'

'Alice, I believe, is asleep. Now, did we not have supper due, sir? I am a little hungry.' Bella thrust her chin in the air. 'I have been waiting . . . above a hour since you disappeared on some . . . sudden business.'

The floorboards creaked as he stepped backwards. Mr Davenport gave a small nod. 'Let us adjourn to supper.'

Bella hesitated with the tray. Mr Davenport came forward and lifted it out of her hands. He strode off in the direction of the stairs. His hair was gleaming and damp curls rested on his cravat at the nape of his neck. It had not been raining outside so he must have had a long ride.

She must ask him what he had been doing — at the earliest opportunity. There had been a pistol shot, and Pamela did not want her brother to know she had been out in the middle of the night.

Hot soup was brought to them straight away. Bella tucked her napkin around her knees and hearing the clink of his spoon against his soup plate, lifted her own spoon keeping her eyes cast down on to the table.

After some time, the girl reappeared to clear away their soup dishes and serve them their next course, topside of beef. Bella dared to steal a glance while the girl was serving.

Mr Davenport was not looking at her, but staring into the distance. Although the beef was delicious she felt she had quite lost her appetite.

And why did he not explain to her what his chasing off into the night was all about?

Once the girl had left the room again, Bella decided she must broach the subject. 'Mr Davenport — '

'You will find the beef is very good,' he said in a matter-of-fact fashion.

She took a small mouthful and nodded. The beef was good and suddenly she felt hungry again.

'Would you like some more red wine?' he added.

Her glass did not really need filling as she had only taken a couple of sips but she nodded. 'Thank you. But . . . ' She really must speak! 'What on earth happened earlier? The pistol shot — '

'You will sometimes find that things are actually more complicated underneath than they first appear to you on the surface.'

'What kind of answer is that?' Bella snapped. 'A riddle?'

'I cannot explain the pistol shot,' he said.

'I am not a feeble miss who needs to be cossetted,' Bella stated.

'No.' He glanced towards the fire. 'I cannot explain the shot, for one thing because I am not wholly sure myself.'

'The ostler said it was a man in a black coat.'

'Yes. It was. I know the man who fired the shot.'

'You do!'

'I do not know why he fired the shot. Although I can guess.' Mr Davenport suddenly pushed his chair back and rose. He walked over to the fireside and leaned his hand against the mantelpiece. 'You say Pamela is fast asleep?'

'I gave her laudanum.'

'Good.' A small smile pushed at the corners of his mouth, then fell away as he glanced down towards her feet tucked below the table. 'Your dress? The hem is torn?'

4

'Yes, it is. And muddied too.' Bella said. 'I was worried. I ran outside.' No untruths there.

He cut a fine figure outlined by the orange glow of the fire but the deep furrow across his brow made something in her chest constrict. She wanted . . . to help him.

'You should not have concerned yourself,' he said in a voice which sounded far too easy. 'All is in hand.'

'But . . . the man with the pistol — '

'The man with the pistol will be dealt with in due course. And is no concern of yours.'

'Is there nothing I can do?' She fingered the linen napkin on her lap. 'To help? Especially after the kindness you and your family have shown to me, I would be only too pleased.'

He looked at her. She could not

make out his thoughts but the expression he was wearing unnerved her and she wondered why she felt disappointed when he simply sat down again and took several large mouthfuls of wine, draining his glass which he immediately refilled.

The situation of being here in this room with him alone and with such conversation struck her as being very intimate. He could have been a husband, standing as he did in front of a fire at their home, sharing his troubled thoughts with her as they dined.

Except that he had not shared his thoughts. She knew nothing more now than she had done before she had asked him. Save that this man who had fired the pistol shot was known to Mr Davenport.

She wondered if she ought to mention to him that she had seen Mr Montcalm, or a man who looked remarkably like him, at the inn earlier. She had better not. There was nothing which led her to suppose that Mr Montcalm had anything to do with the pistol shot, or Pamela's adventure.

Her sigh caught his attention. He looked at her curiously, his fingers feeling the stem of his wine glass. Bella felt heat rising in her cheeks at the knowledge that there was something about this man which attracted her.

The serving girl returned to the room.

Bella hastily ate the currant pudding which was placed before her. Luckily it was well-spiced and tasty and so gave some cover to her embarrassment. She did not look up, but she knew that Mr Davenport's eyes were fixed upon her at every moment.

As soon as she had finished her last mouthful she said, 'Please excuse me' and rushed to remove herself from the table — and him.

'Wait!' She had just reached the door but halted and turned around.

Mr Davenport held his chin and stared at her. 'Will you join me for breakfast?'

Bella found herself nodding.

'I have asked for breakfast to be served here at eight o'clock.'

She nodded again and whispered 'Good night,' as she finally made her escape. She went up to her room and suddenly felt so tired that she went straight to bed.

Bella was surprised how well she slept. She was washed and dressed and still the wooden clock on the mantelpiece above her fire had quarter-of-an-hour to go before eight o'clock. She had dressed herself in what she considered to be her most stylish day dress — a buttermilk muslin.

When it was at last eight, she drew back the bolt from her door slowly and silently. She crept out onto the landing and edged her way to the top of the stairs where she was still invisible to anyone below.

She could hear two gentlemen speaking. She fancied one of them was Mr Davenport but she could not discern the precise words.

57

She began, very quietly, to creep down the stairs one by one, pausing on each to listen and see if she could make out anything being said.

She was hit by the full force of someone coming up the stairs at speed and nearly toppled over had it not been for some strong arms which caught her fall.

Mr Davenport's arms.

He held her upright as she regained her balance. She did not look away but straight into his brown eyes. Finding her gaze returned and in the way he looked at her . . . was he . . . was he going to kiss her?

A harsh shout came from below, 'Davenport!'

'Miss Oakley,' he whispered. 'Some unforeseen circumstances have arisen. If you would be kind enough to wait in your chamber.'

Bella opened her mouth to protest.

'I will send word to you shortly.' There was a serious glint in Mr Davenport's eyes.

Bella nodded and made her way back up the stairs.

Mr Davenport didn't move until she was at the very top of the stairs again. But she wanted to know — was it Mr Montcalm waiting for him downstairs? She could not see and the voices were muted until they disappeared — into one of the rooms. Bella went back to her chamber and paced up and down.

She couldn't just wait. And yet, it was none of her business . . .

She went over to the window and with her body shielded by the thick curtain she watched closely what was happening at the front of the inn. Sure enough Mr Montcalm, wearing the same tan coat as last night came out within a few minutes and one of the stable boys ran to fetch his mount.

His horse was duly led forward and saddled up and Mr Montcalm mounted and rode off. Bella pushed away the wrinkles that had formed on her forehand. Why would Mr Davenport be talking to Mr Montcalm?

A maid knocked on her door and said that breakfast was served.

She found the private dining-room empty, though the breakfast things had been laid out. And there were two jugs with steam escaping from under their lids — fresh coffee and chocolate. She poured herself a cup of coffee, took a piece of toast which she spread with butter.

And waited.

The door opened quietly. 'Good morning,' Mr Davenport said. He was wearing an exquisitely-cut plum-coloured double-breasted riding coat. Its brass buttons glittered, as did his eyes. He moved towards the table and pulled out a chair.

'Good morning, sir.' Bella replied. Had he been wearing the coat on the stairs? She could not recall.

A shaft of pale sunlight filtered through the window and cast squares of light on the tablecloth.

'Despite the impression I may have given to the contrary, I very much enjoyed your company at dinner last night, Miss Oakley.'

'Thank you.' She replied and watched him as he helped himself to some eggs. Beneath his coat he was wearing a pair of buckskin breeches. His black boots looked immaculate with their highly-polished sheen. They had certainly not been near a stable that morning.

'And,' he continued as he strode right over to her, 'my intention this morning is to clear out some cobwebs. After breakfast, will you join me riding?'

Bella ordered her heart to stop racing. It was only to be a ride. She watched him dust his eggs and gammon with black pepper and decided he certainly seemed in good spirits this morning.

'This is one of the better coaching inns,' he said, extracting a piece of toast from the linen in which it had been wrapped. 'I trust your accommodation has been satisfactory?'

'Yes,' Bella replied, wishing she had the wherewithal to think of something further to say. All she could think was that she lacked a looking glass in her room, but if she mentioned this deficiency Mr Davenport might think her vain.

'And the weather,' he continued. 'It would appear to be improving.'

'Ah, yes.'

He spread a scraping of the butter across his toast. 'It would be safe to say that spring is upon us, Miss Oakley. Would you not agree?'

'Yes.'

'Perfectly pleasant for a ride.'

'Yes, Yes . . . please excuse me, Mr Davenport. I shall join you in an hour.'

He nodded his head and smiled.

Why did his smile make her want to blush? Feeling hot as she escaped the dining-room, Bella found her mind was in a muddle. If he was going to say nothing of Mr Montcalm or anything of consequence so be it. But she could still see if Pamela was in sorts.

She rested her cheek on the cool plaster as she tapped on the door of

Pamela's chamber. 'Come in!'

Pamela was sat upright in bed reading and looked resplendent in a porcelain silk chemise and blue Oriental jacket. She looked up from her book. 'Bella!'

'How are you?' Bella ventured.

'Feeling much better now, thank you.' Pamela smiled. Indeed, she did look quite well for someone who had been violently sick and in danger of catching cold the day before.

'I am so sorry for my indisposition,' Pamela said. 'No doubt you are keen to reach London with all speed.'

'It is so kind of you to take me to London,' Bella replied. 'Truly I am in no hurry.'

Pamela laid her book down on the bed. 'I hear you are going out this morning for a ride with my brother?'

Bella felt the beginnings of a blush. Her words had tumbled out like laundry from a basket. 'Yes, it will be lovely.'

'He mentioned of it when he was

here earlier,' Pamela said, tapping her fingers on the book leather. She smiled. 'You enjoy your ride and then I wonder if I am not fit to travel today after all?'

Alice, whom she supposed might have helped her to dress, was nowhere to be found. Bella pinned her hair up without a mirror and fastened her grey riding hat as securely as she could.

When satisfied she was presentable, Bella came downstairs to wait. This was better than pacing about her room and letting her nerves get the better of her. She found a seat tucked behind the door to the main hall in the corner of the main room of the inn.

She heard heavy footsteps come down the stairs. It was Mr Davenport.

He burst into the main room of the inn, his jaw tightly set and wearing a faint frown. 'Ah! Miss Oakley, I see you are ready.'

Bella hastened to her feet.

'Shall we go?' Mr Davenport beckoned towards the door. 'I have arranged a strawberry roan mare for you.'

Bella led the way as he had gestured through the hallway and out of the inn, feeling all the while his heavy presence behind her. It wasn't until she was mounted that she discovered the groom was not to accompany them and they were to ride alone. It was surely improper? She had rather thought that Davies, his valet, would join them.

It seemed too late to protest. And Bella found she didn't want to. Her mare, Christina, was indeed a delightful creature and besides there was the prospect of a good ride, Bella told herself.

Mr Davenport mounted a majestic black stallion by the name of King — the same horse he had cantered out on last night. Bella opened her mouth to say something and then shut it. She was too curious for her own good, and he had already told her all he intended to tell her.

He could have easily outpaced her in both speed and daring, but he did not. He was seemingly content to trot beside her down the narrow lane flanked by fields. It was a cool day — the breeze chilled Bella's face but the hedgerows were bursting with green buds and crouched below them were early daffodils.

They proceeded at a steady pace following a right fork from the lane into some woodland. The ground was firmer and she could again enjoy the sunlight.

Mr Davenport drew King up to her. 'Miss Oakley, it is of course my intention that the correct form should be observed.' He was looking, not at her, but at something at the top of one of the tall beech trees.

'Correct form?' Bella felt herself frown. There was nothing very correct about going for a ride alone with an unmarried gentleman, of that she was sure. 'I am afraid I do not know quite your meaning, sir?'

'You are a little headstrong, are you not?'

Bella gripped her ribbons. 'How . . . how dare you . . . insult me!'

Mr Davenport shook his head. 'You mistake me when I mean rather to compliment you. I find your character . . . rather agreeable. You speak candidly and act firstly with sense.' King jangled his bit. 'I admit surprise, for I expect young ladies not to be so . . . forthright.'

Bella had no notion what to say. He found her character agreeable?

'Allow me to make myself plain,' he continued. He held his reigns in one hand as the other tugged at his cravat. 'For I admit there was a purpose apart from air and exercise for inviting you out to ride.'

King shifted his footing and Mr Davenport held his reigns in both hands again to steady him. 'Nonetheless I would ascertain your feelings on the matter first?'

'My feelings?' She had heard every word of his, had she not? Yet she did not understand what he was saying. Surely . . . ? No! 'Sir, you take the most grievous liberty! My aunt and uncle

67

placed you in a position of trust.'

'So they did,' Mr Davenport said, his voice very dry.

Bella gathered her breath. 'You have no business stepping outside that trust, sir.'

The corners of his mouth twitched. 'Miss Oak — '

'I will and cannot be expected to place myself and my money into your hands for perpetuity, sir.'

His eyebrows raised and then he frowned. And then he laughed.

Heat coursed upwards towards her cheeks and Bella found herself unable to move.

'Is this what you think I am after?' he said. 'Marriage? Well, Miss Oakley, I find the manner in which you rebuff a potential suitor quite refreshing. And, quite in character!'

Bella blinked. Hot tears of embarrassment were pricking at her eyes. A gentle touch on her hand and she looked down to see he was offering her a large gentleman's handkerchief. She took it and blew her nose.

'Might I tell you the reason I wished a tête-à-tête?'

'Please . . . please do,' Bella said swallowing. Christina shifted, impatient at being held so stoutly and Bella forced her grip to relax and looked up.

He was watching her without a flicker of emotion. 'It has not escaped your notice that all is not how it should be. There was good reason I warned you in York of Mr Montcalm. And as you saw — he was also at the inn. A fact I was unaware of until this morning, although it seems he overnighted with us.'

Mr Davenport cleared his throat. 'If you will allow me to be frank. Mr Montcalm may try to approach you. Once I have delivered you to your relatives in London, you are of course free to consort to their dictates, but whilst you are under my protection I ask that you heed my request.

'He is no friend of our family. And I must ask you to be on your guard also for Pamela. She . . . she may not be so

convinced of this necessity. And . . . '
He pulled his sleeve across his brow.
'And there is another gentleman
from whom you should be on your
guard.'

5

Another gentleman? Bella drew herself up in her seat. It had to be the gentleman in the black coat! 'Is the whole of England awash with rogues?' she said lightly. 'I had not credited the journey to London would be so dangerous.'

King snorted. 'Indeed, Miss Oakley.'

Mr Davenport's words were as crisp as boots in new snow. 'Let us return to the inn.'

'But who is this other gentleman?' Bella said turning Christina around. 'Were I a milk-and-water miss, I should be exceedingly alarmed at what you have just told me!'

His eyes fixed on her and his dark lashes swept down as he blinked with the utmost regularity. 'He is the Duke of Markyate, and you are no milk-and-water miss or I should not have spoken.'

He led the way out from the woodland into the open.

'Sir,' Bella began, flattered. 'Am I to assume I am in some kind of danger?'

He looked at her with surprise. 'My dear, you are quite . . . outstanding! I had even gone so far as bringing with me a small vinaigrette of sal volatile borrowed from our landlady in case you had fainted.'

'I have never fainted,' Bella replied. 'That only happens in Gothic novels, or if one is too vain and has one's stays laced too tightly.' She stopped, aware that his eyes had drifted to her waist. Well, her figure was trim enough. But what had prompted her to begin talking to a gentleman about stays!

Back at the inn, Bella hastened upstairs to the solitude of her own room. Why? Why should she think that Mr Davenport meant to offer her marriage?

She changed from her riding dress into a plain white muslin comfortable for easy travelling and packed the rest of her things away.

An hour later they were on the road again, and with Mr Davenport safely hidden behind a newspaper she stared at his buckskin-clad knees and then at the small cracks in the coach leather and considered.

So it seemed there were three gentlemen she must be on her guard from. Mr Montcalm, this mysterious Duke and Mr Davenport.

Mr Davenport's newspaper rustled as he turned the page. He put his newspaper down when they stopped at a turnpike, and appeared in the most temperate of humours.

They were still travelling as darkness began to fall. The coach tumbled off the North road and on to a much narrower road. The coach creaked and swayed.

Pamela, who had been half-asleep, sat up with a jolt. 'Where are we going? Heavens, Anthony! It is getting dark! This road is full of holes!'

'We stop at an inn called *The Pheasant* tonight.' Mr Davenport's voice remained even and undisturbed. 'I sent word ahead. Granted it is a little out of the way, but I am informed the hospitality is superior.'

The hospitality was not superior. After being served a very watery soup, they were served boiled mutton that tasted of shoe leather.

It was nothing she could put her finger on, but Bella wondered why Mr Davenport had chosen to stay at *The Pheasant*. If his objective was to keep away from Mr Montcalm and the Duke, he had succeeded without a doubt. It was hardly a coaching inn at all and they were the only guests.

Bella stamped her feet softly on the ground of the inn yard the next morning. No-one would hear this in the clatter of the coach being brought around. She wriggled her toes in her boots. It was chillier than yesterday. The March wind was in force against the new budded tree branches.

'Miss Oakley?'

Bells started at his deep voice. Mr

Davenport wore a smile as he strode around the coach towards her, immaculate in his buckskin breeches and sober black jacket.

'Would you like to join me up top?' he said. 'I am in a humour to show off my skills at the ribbons.'

Bella's first instinct was to refuse. It would be far warmer inside the coach than without on a day like today. But she had often wondered what it would be like to perch on the top of a carriage like a tiger.

'Yes,' she said. 'Yes, please.'

Mile after mile flew past. They came through a village where she watched a woman leading a gaggle of geese up the road and a group of children playing around a lumbering and ancient oak tree. Then they were out into the open countryside again and with a clear road ahead the horses were able to settle into a regular stride.

Mr Davenport spoke for the first time. 'The weather threatens to be inclement.'

'You think it might rain?' Bella ventured.

He looked up briefly at the sky. 'I wonder what you think of me, Miss Oakley?'

'Think of you? Oh, I do not think — '

'You are blushing,' he said as if they were still discussing the weather. 'So what has been occupying your thoughts? The scenery?'

'Yes.'

He tipped his head back and laughed. 'Let us talk instead about the delights of Cambridgeshire through which we are to pass this afternoon? Have you ever visited Newmarket, Miss Oakley?'

'No, this is my first time further south than York.'

He flicked the ribbons. 'The races at Newmarket are quite splendid. Were it possible, I would take you there myself, for you would enjoy it.'

Bella ignored the heavy feeling in her stomach and kept her voice bright. 'Newmarket is superior to London?'

'Newmarket is organised for sport, and can be most diverting. London is governed by Society. It can be very tiresome.'

'I am looking forward to the balls and seeing the Palace of Westminster.'

'Miss Oakley, as you are wont to ever remind me, you have not been to London before. It will engage you utterly at first. But the splendour will fade and the parties become monotonous.' He sounded wistful, as if he was remembering better days, or wishing it were different.

'I shall make the most of my time in London,' Bella said. 'After that it will depend on my husband's circumstances and I cannot say whether or not I shall visit again.'

'Miss Oakley, do you think me old?'

'Sir, I have not your meaning?'

'I am nine and twenty, and you are . . . ?'

'Eighteen.'

'Eighteen,' he repeated, not flinching his gaze from the road ahead.

'No,' Bella ventured, 'Nine and twenty is not old.'

She watched the way the wind blew into his greatcoat and moulded it to the form of his body. He flicked the ribbons in absolute control and she remembered how he lifted the trunks down from the carriage with ease.

The silence between them seemed to grow and as it grew it became increasingly oppressive. There was no comfort or escape from the openness of the outside.

The sky had grown darker and the wind become harsher. It was getting colder. Bella gripped her hands together tightly in her lap and tried not to shiver.

'We must press on,' Mr Davenport said as if he could read her thoughts. 'Past Newark.'

Bella felt a drop of rain on her nose and looked up at the leaden sky.

'Confound it!' Mr Davenport said as the rain began to fall.

He drove the horses hard but they were in open countryside. There was no shelter in sight. Bella felt the rain start to seep through her clothes and rubbed her arms. The wind continued to batter and chill.

'Ah ha!' Mr Davenport shouted as they came over the brow of a hill and not half a mile ahead was a village.

Bella shut her eyes and didn't open them until they stopped. They were outside the front door of an inn, its sign swinging frantically so she could not see its name.

Mr Davenport helped her down. His hands were warm even through the wet glove leather.

'Go straight in and sit by the fire!'

Fuming at his high-handedness Bella wanted to say something in return, but she stopped herself. She gripped her skirts up above her ankles and avoiding the puddles ran into the inn.

There was a roaring fire in the inn's private sitting-room and the landlady at once brought them towels and a pot of tea.

The door opened and Mr Davenport, who must have removed his sodden greatcoat elsewhere, came in. He cast his eyes about the room and the landlady stopped pouring the tea and curtsied.

'We will overnight here,' he said.

'Very good sir,' she replied. 'I'll have fires lit upstairs right away.'

He nodded and left then with a swish of his dark coat tails, but without another word.

The rain beat on the small leaded windowpanes of the room.

'He's in a temper,' Pamela said and helped herself to a piece of honey cake. 'Is this baked today?'

'Yes, miss,' the landlady replied.

'It looks delicious. Bella, do you want a piece?'

Bella helped herself and then sat down in a chair. It was rather old and the horsehair had become lumpy. She shifted and tried to make herself comfortable. Just when she thought she had the measure of the man, he confused her again. Why on earth should Mr Davenport be in a temper?

Later they dined alone, the inn being empty of any other guests. Mr Davenport remained rather subdued with a thoughtful expression and only spoke when it was necessary. Bella wondered if he was a little melancholy or whether he was simply weary.

He excused himself from their company the moment it was polite to do so.

'Let us retire too.' Pamela yawned. 'Isabella, I have a most informative book on domestic economy if you were in want of something to read?'

Bella rose from her chair refusing to think if this was another reference to Pamela's hopes for a match between her and her brother.'

'I find it useful to be prepared,' Pamela added. 'And every wife should aim to excel at household management.'

Bella saw in her mind Mr Davenport splendidly arrayed as he came to church on his wedding day. And beside him she stood, in a most beautiful wedding dress made, it would seem, almost wholly from the finest lace.

Mr Davenport would doubtless excel at being a fine husband — when he found the right woman to be his bride.

Bella said in a clear voice she hoped expressed no emotion. 'Yes, I should be delighted to borrow the volume.'

Next morning Bella woke to find her throat was very dry and her head heavy. She poured herself a cup of water and opened one of the leaded-glass windows to allow some fresh air into the room.

She had a piece of toast and coffee and felt a little better as she set about her packing. She had just finished when there was a knock at the door and Alice informed her they were planning to leave in about quarter-of-an-hour.

Bella checked she had not forgotten anything before closing her trunk. She tucked two clean handkerchiefs into her reticule and came downstairs.

She stepped outside to see the coach being prepared in the yard and told Mr

Davies her trunk was ready.

'Very good, miss,' he said and went with the other of the Davenports' male servants to fetch it.

After a few minutes, there being no sign of Mr Davenport or Pamela, Bella went back into the inn.

She pushed open the stout front door and lifted the iron latch of the thinner inner door and pulled it open. The front door thudded shut as a voice said, 'Miss Oakley?'

A man's voice.

She stepped fully into the hall to see the figure. Mr Montcalm!

The inner door creaked shut behind her.

Bella nodded. If she acknowledged him only by sight and did not speak she might be able to disappear upstairs without appearing too ill-mannered.

He moved so that he was standing in front of the bottom of the staircase. Her escape route was blocked. Bella shivered. Mr Davenport had said there was no danger, and yet the back of her neck prickled.

'Miss Oakley,' he effused. 'What a coincidence to meet you here on your way to London! Has your journey been satisfactory?'

She could not help but answer him. 'Yes, sir. Tolerable.'

He moved a step closer to her and she could smell his strong cologne. 'You will be in demand over the next few weeks, but if you will allow me to call on you . . . ?'

A wave of panic hit and Bella felt light in the head. What was Mr Montcalm doing here? Surely it could not be a coincidence?

'Miss Oakley has no wish to renew your acquaintance.' The low measured voice was Mr Davenport's. He came into the hallway from the main room and stood tall by her side.

The look that passed from him to Mr Montcalm was like a thrown dagger.

'Perhaps,' Mr Montcalm said softly. 'Miss Oakley might be allowed to speak for herself?'

There was a tension in the air as

thick as a blanket and all she could think was what Mr Davenport was going to say next. After a pause, which seemed to last an age in the stony silence he said, 'Miss Oakley is under my protection and on this occasion, I think not.'

The unwanted attentions of Mr Montcalm were bad enough, but she was a lady with her own mind, not a servant to be ordered around as he chose! Yet Bella had not the least idea how to protest. She stared at the knots in the floor as if their pattern would somehow give her inspiration.

'Come,' Mr Davenport's voice held a lighter tone but it still suggested his authority was not to be challenged — by anyone. 'The coach is ready.'

6

Bella placed her kid-gloved hand on Mr Davenport's proffered arm. It was warm and steady. She knew she was relieved he had rescued her, but her crossness also bit at her chest. She looked up and smiled at him to make sure Mr Montcalm could not guess that anything might be amiss.

Mr Montcalm's eyes seemed amused. That she did not understand. He stepped back out of their way with a tight nod and let them pass.

The coach, of course, was not quite ready, but Mr Davenport stood and talked to her about some of the occasions a young lady would enjoy in London, the balls, the opera, the parties and routs, and she could not help but be interested, although she knew that he was doing it so that she had no opportunity to escape from his immediate presence.

They set off about half-an-hour later. Mr Davenport announced that they were to cover a good few miles today and that he was going to ride out. Sure enough they made good progress, passing through Huntingdon and then St Neots where they stopped for refreshments.

They continued on from St Neots with Mr Davenport joining them in the coach. There was little conversation and Pamela looked particularly pensive.

They finally reached Baldock and their overnighting place, *The George*, just before five o'clock.

Bella hesitated in the hall tempted to excuse herself too and save herself from having to dine alone with Mr Davenport. However, *The George* was the grandest inn they had stayed in so far, so they would be dining with company and when the landlord came out from one of the far doors so did wonderful cooking smells.

She went up to her room. It was very spacious and had its own desk. She had time to write a letter to Aunt Harriet before getting dressed for dinner.

She turned in front of the mirror and regarded herself critically. The mulberry was one of her favourite dresses as the colour seemed to well suit her complexion. She touched the delicate muslin and the fine Nottingham lace on her sleeves.

It was time she started to behave like a real lady as this was the role she would have to pull off in the weeks ahead. She imagined that she was Pamela and held her chin high. She carried herself out of her room walking correctly as if she had a heavy volume balanced on her head and down the stairs. There was no one to see and her heartbeats subsided a little.

The floorboards creaked as someone stepped out of the shadows.

'Miss Oakley?'

It was Mr Davenport. He offered her his arm. How steadfast it felt! If only all their encounters could be as simple as this.

It turned out to be quite a formal dinner. It was the first time she had dined with such company without her aunt and uncle. Up till now the Davenports had tended to prefer small establishments off the main road. *The George* was different, a busy coaching inn.

The company consisted of a Major and Mrs Crossley, an elderly couple on their way to London from Cambridgeshire and Mrs Paxton-Claremont, a formidable lady with her daughter Celia, travelling to London from Lancashire.

It appeared that the Davenports and Paxton-Claremonts were already of an acquaintance and Mr Davenport was vociferous in striking up suitable and lively conversation with both mother and daughter.

Miss Paxton-Claremont was a picture of feminine delicacy with her perfect guinea golden curls, small button nose and powder blue silk evening gown reflecting her porcelain complexion.

Bella felt her chest constrict as she

watched Miss Paxton-Claremont laugh at something Mr Davenport said. Why did Mr Davenport so clearly favour Miss Paxton-Claremont with the majority of his remarks and questions?

If only her hair, instead of being dark and difficult to manage, could be golden like Miss Paxton-Claremont's. If only her eyes could be blue instead of brown. If only her features could be delicate and well-proportioned. Miss Paxton-Claremont would have no trouble in finding a gentleman to fall in love with her in London, Bella was sure.

After dinner Mrs Paxton-Claremont suggested a game of cards, but no-one was keen to take her up on the offer, particularly not her daughter who was now in the advantageous position of having Mr Davenport at her right hand and presumably had no wish to bring a premature end to this arrangement.

'Well, we might as well turn in as I am feeling tired,' announced Mrs Paxton-Claremont.

Miss Paxton-Claremont moved a

step farther into the sitting-room. 'Oh, you go ahead, Mama. I will be up very shortly.'

Not a moment after she had gone Mr Davenport rose from his seat by the far window and came to sit beside Miss Paxton-Claremont. His muted whisper to her was lost in a sudden crackle of the fire.

Miss Paxton-Claremont smothered a giggle. Bella turned away and caught Pamela's eye.

'I am remarkably tired,' Pamela said. Her skirts rustled as she stood up. 'I think I shall also go to bed.'

'Oh, don't tease so,' Miss Paxton-Claremont's sugared voice exclaimed.

Bella swallowed the lump in her throat. How could he flirt so flagrantly? She was embarrassed. What a lucky escape she had had! To think she had developed soft feelings for this man! And considered him a gentleman!

'And I. Goodnight.' Bella kept her eyes cast to the floor as she hastened out of the room in Pamela's wake.

Bella turned her pillow over and tried again to get to sleep. The bed was not uncomfortable. She was not cold. But she was finding it difficult to sleep.

The night's silence was piercing. There were no sounds of carousing from downstairs or the scuffle of traffic outside.

Somewhere a long way distant she heard a dog bark.

An owl hooted.

There was a creak of wood.

Someone was opening her door!

Bella found she couldn't move. The door opened slowly and she heard breathing. Then the footstep as the person entered her room.

Tall, he stood as a hazy silhouette for a moment in the doorway before stepping forward — coming directly towards her!

Bella wanted to scream. Her throat refused to make a sound.

He stepped into the shaft of moonlight which set his eyes glinting. And showed his face.

Mr Montcalm!

'Pamela?' he whispered.

With a mighty effort and as much noise as possible, Bella sat up in bed. She pulled the counterpace right up to her neck and forced her voice to be loud. 'Mr Montcalm, get out of my bedchamber!'

He froze, and panic flittered across his eyes. Bella breathed very deeply and willed her heart to stop racing. He was in the wrong. He was a gentleman. He would go away.

For a moment nothing happened. Then he pulled at his cravat. 'Indeed, madam, I am terribly sorry to have chanced upon you in this way. To whom should I apologise?'

Of course, it was so dark where she was he could not recognise her! Bella felt a surge of relief. 'Sir,' she said, pitching her voice higher than natural, 'have a thought to propriety and please leave my chamber.'

He hesitated and then, without a word left the room, closing her door behind him.

Bella flew out of bed and turned the key in the doorlock. She stopped with her back against the cold door and listened to the thud of her heart. Mr Montcalm had come into her room.

Mr Montcalm had come into her room thinking it was Pamela's. Where would he go next? Pamela's room . . .

Bella rushed over to her trunk and stubbed her toe. She stopped herself crying out.

Her fingers were trembling as she unlocked her door. Pamela was only next door but Bella knew she should not be stepping out into the corridor of a public inn in the middle of the night, and undressed.

The corridor was unlit but there was enough light from the window at the end to see her way. She tapped on Pamela's door very gently. There was no answer. She tried the handle. The door was locked.

Was Pamela safe asleep inside . . . Or . . . ?

Bella could not stop thinking of the night when she'd found Pamela out in the orchard. Mr Montcalm had been at that inn, along with the Duke with the pistol. There was something very shady going on, and it involved Pamela Davenport.

She rapped her knuckles on the door again, as loudly as she dared. Her heart thudded in her ears.

A warm male hand rested itself around her wrist. 'Hush!' said Mr Davenport, standing so close behind her she could feel the heart and hear the rise and fall of his chest. He whispered, 'There is a connecting door from your chamber, is there not?'

Bella nodded. Of course there was, hidden behind a thick curtain. Why had she not thought? Mr Davenport removed his hand from hers and allowed her to inch past him and lead the way. Her cheeks were flaming and her fingers felt cold. Not only had Mr Davenport seen her in her wrapper and with bare feet, but his bare hand had touched hers.

And now he was coming into her bedchamber.

He shut the door behind him and locked it. 'You will have to forgive the indiscretion of my entering your bed-chamber, but . . .'

Bella nodded. Pamela was in danger and he knew it.

He crept over to the heavy curtain and drew it back. Bella stayed a way behind, next to her bed, and watched. He silently turned the door handle.

Thud, thud, thud — the sound of someone running across the floor. Bella stopped breathing. The click of a lock. The creak of a door.

Mr Davenport crashed into Pamela's room.

A taper had been lit. Its orange light filtered in her room. Bella followed.

Pamela was stood at her door, having just let Mr Montcalm in. A candle stood burning on her dresser.

'Montcalm,' Mr Davenport said with anger simmering just below the surface, 'you go too far.'

'I fear it is you who has intruded on this scene,' Mr Montcalm replied, his voice smooth as butter. 'Ah, Miss Oakley. It was you I compromised earlier.'

'Sir!' Bella stifled her cry with her hand.

'Indeed.' Mr Davenport turned to face her. There appeared to be nothing in his eyes or written on his face. No emotion, only coldness. 'Miss Oakley there is no requirement for your presence. Please return to your chamber.'

A look of surprise flickered across Mr Montcalm's face. His eyes narrowed. 'Ah, I did not realise yours was the prior claim — '

'Enough!' Pamela said shaking her hands.

Mr Davenport blinked. 'Sister — '

Mr Montcalm broke in with a laugh.

Mr Davenport's eyes darkened to thunder. 'You will not slander a lady in my presence, Montcalm.'

Mr Montcalm squared back his shoulders. 'The fact remains that I spent some time in Miss Oakley's bedchamber — '

Mr Davenport sprang forward. In

one move he had Mr Montcalm's collars in his fists and his body backed up against the wall.

'You will not get the better of me on this one, Montcalm. She is nothing to me but a piece of very mediocre origins I have undertaken to deliver to her family in London. Now, the choice is yours. Leave here immediately and say nothing or there will be the devil to pay!'

Bella stumbled backwards and found her way back into her own room. She shut the door. Locked both doors. Climbed into bed and listened to the muted voices, whose words she could not discern, until all became quiet again.

She didn't care about Pamela or Mr Montcalm or the Duke with the pistol, or anything else clandestine that was going on. None of it mattered because tomorrow she would come to London and her journey with the Davenports would be over.

Thankfully she must have got to sleep not too much later. The morning passed very quickly and Bella spent the time in the company of the Major and his wife until the coach was ready to depart.

The day was fine with sunshine, though the air was crisp. Mr Davenport had elected to outride again which meant they could talk about fashions and things of ladies' interest inside the coach. And Bella found she wanted to talk, and she was pleased that Pamela seemed animated and yet made no mention of the events of the night before.

There was a bustle about the countryside as they drew nearer to London and much more traffic on the road.

'I shall have to scoop myself a decent offer,' Pamela said. She looked quite resplendent sat back against the blue velvet squabs in her day gown of buff-coloured fine cambric. 'No-one minds a chit not getting hitched on her first season. But she needs to bag the game in seasons two or three or otherwise she is in danger of being well and truly left on the shelf.'

Bella smiled and nodded. Yet she was plain Miss Oakley, not a person of fashion like Pamela Davenport. What were the real odds of her making a good match?

They were soon both distracted as they came into London itself. Bella stared out as they drove past market gardens and villas until the streets were lined with terraced housing punctuated by inns and shops. Eventually the streets became finer, the houses larger and there were squares with gardens in the middle.

'This is the West End,' Pamela said. 'Nearly there.'

Brook Street was a street of fine houses in a mixture of styles and Bella somewhat overawed when they entered the gates of one of the grandest houses in the street. This was the home of her cousins, the Cavenhams! For the next few weeks this would be her home. Was the Davenport's London house as fine as this?

Two footman appeared and one of them handed her down. Pamela followed on. They were ushered up the sweeping stone stairs that led to the imposing black front door. Before she had even reached the top of the stairs a grand lady swept out of the house. Bella knew at once it must be her Aunt Clarissa.

Clarissa Cavenham was slim and elegant in her buttercup coloured day dress. She stood waiting by the door as Bella made her progress up the stairs. 'Isabella! I am so delighted you have finally made it to us safely.'

Bella placed her hands in her aunt's. 'Aunt Clarissa, I am so happy to meet you.'

'Do come in and tell us what took you so long to get to London, we were almost getting worried!' Aunt Clarissa leaned forward and whispered, 'I heard the Davenports had come to your aid. Your uncle wrote and gave all the details. Is there any news I should know of?'

Bella turned her face away. Her cheeks felt hot. Her aunt was making it clear a girl in her position ought to take advantage of every opportunity which presented itself.

Clarissa let her go and nodded at Pamela who had come up behind them. 'Miss Davenport, I haven't seen you for quite a while, perhaps not since last year? You do look well. That northern air has quite put some colour in your cheeks.'

Pamela smiled. 'Yes, we had a wonderful winter in Yorkshire — '

'I am afraid my sister is a little tired after our long journey.' Mr Davenport had dismounted and stood at the bottom of the steps. 'We must trouble you no longer.'

Aunt Clarissa smiled and waved at him. 'Mr Davenport, I congratulate you. You have delivered your charge successfully and appear to me to be young man already able to step into your father's shoes.'

Clarissa looked across at Bella and

smiled. 'No doubt Isabella will fill me in on all the details of the journey, and you are quite right, we must not detain you any longer. You must be tired and wanting to get home.'

'Thank you very much for delivering me safely, sir.' Bella looked past the curl of his dark hair against his white cravat, past his firm chin and long nose and to his eyes.

His eyes swept away and he nodded at her aunt. Then Mr Davenport turned away. She watched the sweep of his creaseless superfine jacket, heard his boots on the gravel as he strode away back towards the coach and out of her life.

7

Although Aunt Clarissa had assured her that this evening was to be a small intimate affair, there were to be twelve people at dinner. Bella sat as Molly, who was to be her own personal maid, finished arranging her hair.

She kept her hands clasped tightly in her lap and tried to remain absolutely still and not think of what was ahead. Rather, she considered the Chinese pattern which was papered on the walls of her chamber. Long-legged birds, which looked like herons, stood among the reeds.

The wardrobes had turned out to contain a number of dresses which far exceeded in quality and fashion any she currently possessed, and she was excited to discover that these had been ordered and made up for her. Her maid was now busy making little alterations where they were needed.

Bella was surprised to see that of all the people in London, the company included Mrs and Miss Paxton-Claremont whom she had dined with only yesterday. They were accompanied by Mr Paxton-Claremont and their son, George.

Also present were the Duke and Duchess of Stanbridge, a Mr and Mrs Fitzwilliam and a young member of parliament, Sir Edward Forresby.

Mrs Paxton-Claremont greeted her most warmly and Bella was glad of an acquaintance to talk to among so many strangers. She wondered how far these guests were selected for her benefit when Aunt Clarissa instructed George Paxton-Claremont that he could have the privilege of taking her into dinner. She found herself sat between him and the seemingly illustrious Sir Edward Forresby.

Miss Paxton-Claremont, however, was sat at Sir Edward's left and succeeded in gaining the majority of that young man's attention, leaving her to make do with her less than talkative brother. Fortified by at least one glass of wine, Bella decided she should try to join in the general conversation.

'Too many confounded Whigs. That's the problem,' Mr Fitzwilliam said with a sniff.

'Excuse me gentlemen, but this is not a political salon!' Aunt Clarissa said very loudly.

'However, I must just clear my name, especially in the presence of such charming ladies who could get the wrong idea.' Sir Edward beamed at her and Miss Paxton-Claremont. 'I am not a Whig.'

Bella was not sure exactly what a Whig was, except that it was a type of politician. A club they joined or something.

'Nor are you a Tory!' The Duke added. There was laughter.

That was the other side, the Tories. So what was Sir Forresby? It seemed like a good question so she decided to ask. 'Excuse me, Sir Forresby.'

Every one of the twenty-two eyes of the people around the table turned to her.

'If you are not a Whig or a Tory, what are you?'

'Dammed good question.' Mr Fitzwilliam applauded. 'That debate would certainly liven things up at Whites.'

There was more laughter. Bella was sure she had gone bright crimson. George Paxton-Claremont whispered something in her ear. 'They are laughing because Whites is above party politics.'

'Bella, dear sweet girl,' Aunt Clarissa said in the hearing of the whole company. 'We really must get you filled in on the subject of politics. Sir Edward, perhaps you could instruct our guest a little?'

'And ruin that charming innocence?' replied Sir Edward, dabbing the sides of his mouth with his napkin.

Bella was amazed at how such artless ignorance on her part could be considered so charming, but if that was all it took to gain London's attention, she could do that.

'Thank you, Sir Forresby, I would be most obliged.' Bella fluttered her eyelashes at him, directly copying how she had seen it done by Miss Paxton-Claremont on several occasions.

That was how the conversation went in London. Never had she heard so many grown-up people round a table being quite so loud and ill-mannered to each other. She had imagined dinners in London to be grand models of perfection.

Later, after the guests had departed, Aunt Clarissa was adamant that the evening had been a complete success. She sat down next to Bella in the drawing-room. 'My dear, one intimate dinner at home and both Mr Paxton-Claremont and Sir Edward have asked if they could call! You shall have the pick of the best of them. I am quite convinced.'

Bella forced herself to smile. Her aunt patted her hand. 'Drawing up your list will be a straightforward pleasure.'

'List?'

'I shall write a list of acceptable gentlemen. It is useful to let people know who is in the running and at what level we are pitching ourselves.'

Bella shuddered. 'But where is the romance in choosing a husband from a piece of paper?'

'Oh, my dear child!' Aunt Clarissa chuckled. 'You need not worry. My three daughters were all betrothed in their first season. Every mama worth her salt has a list. The absence of one would indicate a lack of planning or ambition. And your mama would have wanted the best for you.'

'Yes. Yes, of course.'

'But remember . . . ' Aunt Clarissa's brow furrowed. 'Simply because a gentleman is named on the list does not mean consent for your hand has been given. Circumstances can change. On the other hand, there may be opportunities the list does not cover — a younger son suddenly inherits, a foreign aristocrat newly arrived in town. Every eventuality cannot be foreseen.'

'No. No, of course not.' Bella shook her head.

'And also, you should be aware that the list may contain some names which through family and friendship loyalties we are obliged to include, but you should not feel you have to give them serious consideration.'

'Do you mean like Mr Paxton-Claremont?' Bella asked.

Aunt Clarissa gave her an appraising look. 'Be sure of one thing, Isabella. What with your unusual beauty, your obvious charms, innocence and money, you are fit for any of them. Yes indeed, any of them. Now, it is late, my sweet child. Be off to bed and leave everything to me.'

Aunt Clarissa rose from the sofa.

What about Sir Edward Forresby? Bella wondered. Was he on the list? Or Mr Davenport? It was too late to ask — Aunt Clarissa was already at the drawing-room door.

Bella rose and followed her. Why did her heart suddenly feel heavy as she thought about Mr Davenport? What was he doing now, at this very moment? Up late after dinner, or gone out to a club or perhaps early to bed?

Bella was up the following morning by eight o'clock. She came downstairs eager for the day ahead, but found the dining-room deserted of people and food. Was there some other arrangement for taking breakfast of which she was not aware? She paused and turned to leave the room when a maid rushed into the dining-room and stifled a gasp with her hand as she saw Bella.

'Has everyone breakfasted already?'

'No, Miss.' The maid bobbed a small curtsey. 'We usually lay out at ten-thirty.'

Ten-thirty! Everyone must still be asleep.

Bella left the empty dining-room and wondered how she would occupy herself for the next couple of hours. Venturing out of the house was out of the question.

Bella opened a door which she discovered led to a sitting-room or perhaps a morning-room. Where was the library?

It was beyond the drawing-room. Mahogany shelves lined the walls from floor to ceiling of the small, but not inconsequential room, and in the middle were three armchairs and a table on which various papers and magazines were laid.

Top of the pile was *The Morning Post*. She took the paper quickly. She knew it was not quite the thing for a young lady to be interested in anything except the court and social pages so while she was alone she would make the most of it.

Newspapers were written for gentlemen by gentlemen, although it was acceptable for short exerts, suitably rephrased where necessary for the limitations of the female mind, to be read aloud in female company. It was supposed that subjects such as the war or the government were only of limited interest.

However, Aunt Harriet was interested and together they had been following the vilified Emperor Napoleon's campaigns.

'Good morning!'

Bella dropped the paper. 'Mr Cavenham! Good morning!'

'Reading the newspaper, eh? Bit of a bluestocking are you? And do call me Charles.' He fingered his chin and stepped into the room.

Bella picked the newspaper up from the carpet.

'You should first read this.' Charles sauntered over and pulled a large volume from the shelves. 'Burke's.'

Charles handed her the volume and took the newspaper. 'Read that and then you'll understand *The Morning Post*. Everyone's in there.'

'Thank you . . . Charles.'

Bella opened the volume on her lap. It claimed to detail all the peers in the realm. She found Cavenham. Henry John Marmaduke Cavenham, fifth Earl of Waverley. The Hon Charles who sat behind the paper was there. And their parents, the fourth Earl.

In fact, detailed was the whole family line back to the first Earl who was given the peerage at the time of the Restoration. She then found the Duke and Duchess of Stanbridge whom she had met at dinner last night, but she found nothing under Paxton-Claremont or Forresby. Sir Edward must have been awarded his knighthood recently.

She could not stop herself turning to see if there was a Davenport. She did not expect to find anything and she was proved right. There were no Davenports. Bella snapped the book shut.

Charles looked up from his paper. 'Heavy going, eh?'

'Quite the contrary.' Bella replied. 'Everyone I know isn't in it.'

Charles shrugged. 'Now you're here in town, my girl, that'll change.'

Bella put Burke's back in its place on the shelf and selected one of the magazines, entitled *The Ladies' Magazine*. She was pleasantly diverted by the fashion plates for about an hour before they were disturbed.

A tall, dark-haired young lady dressed in apricot silk with a sealskin pelisse walked straight into the library, quite unannounced.

Charles put down his paper, and rising, said, 'Jane, dearest. What brings you here so early?'

'Why, to meet my newest cousin of course!'

This was Lady Jane Cavenham, only daughter of the Earl of Waverley! Aunt Harriet had always spoken of her as if she was a little girl, but Lady Jane was a young lady, of at least her own age. And she looked as if she had stepped straight out from one of the magazine plates!

Jane turned to face her. 'Until a few weeks ago, cousin Isabella, I hardly knew of your existence. And now you are here with us in London!'

'I am very pleased to meet you, cousin Jane.' Bella took her hands.

'Enough of this cousin business, for surely you have many already. I am simply Jane, and shall be your dearest friend.' She turned to Charles. 'Have you breakfasted?'

Charles shook his head.

'Uncle, the hours kept in this house are, I declare, quite shocking. We always breakfast at nine. Later than that and you have to face a cold tray and the wrath of Papa.'

'Indeed,' Charles replied, 'So are you to join us for breakfast, or not?'

'I might be able to find room for a morsel of toast. I came to ask if Isabella would like to join me this morning. I intend to go to Bond Street on some errands. I thought that Isabella might be in need of some bits and pieces.'

Bond Street was only a short walk. There seemed to be plenty of people about, not just shopkeepers and trades-men, but fashionably-dressed ladies, daughters with their mamas, and gentlemen of varying ages, alone or in groups, going to and fro between the shops, or stopping to talk to acquain-tances or to take refreshment in one of the coffee houses.

James, the footman who was with them, opened the door to the haberdashers where Jane, after much consideration, purchased twelve small mother of pearl buttons for some evening gloves.

'If you want to see what London is really like we should go to St James Street, but we cannot chance the scandal.'

'Scandal?' Bella asked.

'It is not really done for young ladies, in fact ladies of any age or reputation, to be wandering down St James Street without some very specific purpose, lest we be in mortal danger from the proliferation of idle Dandies and Bucks.'

Bella laughed.

'This,' Jane said stopping outside a fine façade, 'is Mr John Weston's premises. Again, probably stuffed with Rakes so it would not be prudent for us to step inside.'

'Mr Weston?'

'He is England's finest tailor. His

customers include Mr Beau Brummell and the Prince of Wales himself.'

'Lady Cavenham!'

Jane turned, her eyes widening. 'Your Grace!'

A tall man, with all the aplomb of an army general, but without an ounce of spare flesh on him, stood behind them. There was not a speck of dust on him or out of place fold. His cravat looked so stiff as to be painful.

'My pleasure.' He took Jane's dainty gloved hand and brushed its back with his lips in a careful flourish.

'May I present my cousin and dearest friend?' Small spots of colour arrived in Jane's cheeks. 'Miss Isabella Oakley. Isabella, His Grace, The Duke of Markyate.'

Bella felt herself blink. She closed her mouth and forced a smile. He was so ... handsome. She'd imagined the Duke with the pistol might have a hooked nose or a scar across his face. And cruel eyes.

His eyes danced with amusement and

charisma. 'Delighted to make your acquaintance, Miss Oakley.'

'How do you do, sir.' Bella gave a small curtsey.

He turned back to face Jane and bowed. 'Your servant.'

His Grace took his leave of them.

'Is he not remarkably handsome?' Jane's voice was very soft. 'A veritable Corinthian. I wonder . . . '

She didn't continue what she was saying. Bella touched her sleeve. 'Who, Jane?'

Jane gave a little sigh. 'In truth, there are only four men in London worth marrying and I suppose I shall have to make my mind up soon.'

'Only four?'

'Yes. The Duke of Markyate, Lord Caterton, Sir Edward Forresby and Mr Anthony Davenport.'

A sharp breeze stung Bella's cheek. She turned against the wind. Her cousin Jane was considering marrying Mr Davenport. But wait? Jane had also mentioned the Duke of Markyate.

'The Duke of Markyate?' Bella forced herself to say, and tried to remove all thoughts of Mr Davenport from her mind. The Duke of Markyate — the Duke with the black coat — was the Duke with the pistol. She should try and find out what she could about him.

'Yes, he is top of my list,' Jane replied. 'The most eligible man in England! Unfortunately everyone, including the Duke himself, knows it. Lord Caterton is nearly as eligible, so I may have to settle for him. Sir Edward Forresby is quite a catch, but I wager he might be too clever for me.'

'Oh?' Bella muttered, struggling to think how she could turn the conversation back to the Duke.

'It is said that he will one day be Prime Minister,' Jane continued. 'And Mr Davenport is simply the most dashing young buck in town, and of good character.'

Bella wriggled her fingers in her gloves. Why was Mr Davenport indeed so eligible? He was rich, and handsome, but he was not a Duke or a Lord, not destined to become Prime Minister.

Jane stamped her feet. 'It is cold, let us walk back towards Brook Street.'

'Tell me,' Bella said as they hurried away from Mr Weston's, 'why is it that Mr Davenport should be esteemed so highly as to be included in such a list of notables such as the Duke of Markyate?'

'But, Bella, you know the Davenports! You travelled to London with them! Tell me rather what did you think of Mr Davenport?'

'Mr Davenport . . . ' Bella looked down at the grey pavement. 'Mr Davenport . . . is . . . a gentleman.'

'He is a gentleman and he is the heir now since his elder brother was killed in Spain.'

'Oh!' Mrs Sinclair had mentioned something of this in York, but Bella did not know the particulars.

'It was some time ago, five or six years perhaps.' Jane shrugged. 'There are always those lost in wars.'

'Yes . . . ' Bella found she knew not what else to say.

'However, I seem to recall there is some kind of understanding between Mr Davenport and Miss Paxton-Claremont.'

'Oh?'

'Miss Paxton-Claremont is admired by all gentlemen quite collectively and universally. But her papa, a major in the light dragoons, expired during the battle of Talavera. They have sold their place in South Audley Street and have taken a house in Brompton!'

Jane shook her head. 'She must marry well this season. I would not be surprised if the cost of another season is beyond them.'

It was a stark thought, that behind all the elegance of society were some people who were gambling everything on a successful outcome. Bella suddenly felt very privileged, not just to have been given the opportunity to come to London, but that she had a choice in all of it.

If she failed to find a husband here, there would still be opportunities for her in Hexham. Oh! But how disappointed everyone would be! She must not fail them.

8

What with Jane's enthusiasm and Aunt Clarissa's diligence, Bella did not get a moment to herself over the next few days. It was so busy that she had to especially request half-an-hour to herself to have time to write to Aunt Harriet.

That afternoon she had stayed at home with Aunt Clarissa to receive calls. Six different sets of visitors came to the house and stayed anything from ten minutes to half an hour. They were all new to her save one, Sir Edward Forresby, who was the ten-minute visitor. It was enough that he had visited at all explained Clarissa later. Gentlemen tended towards shorter calls, Clarissa had said. They had little interest in female conversation.

Bella had been indignant for a moment. Mr Davenport had been interested in more than ten minutes of conversation with her. And he was not even interested in her by way of . . .

Nevertheless, Sir Edward was an esteemed catch. To have snared his interest at all was quite a thing. She decided not to worry to give much thought to Sir Edward per se. He was just an admirer. The time was not yet that she should worry of her own feelings on the matter.

The following morning she slept in late. They had attended a small soiree given by a certain Lady Barcleywood, but a couple of sets for dancing had been got up and Mr Gray, Lady Barcleywood's nephew and a mild mannered young man, had proved to be a rather energetic dancing partner.

It was Aunt Clarissa's day for calling, so in the afternoon they went around a number of houses and finally to the Countess of Waverley's. Bella's spirits rose as she saw that Lady Jane was also there to receive them.

'Cousin Isabella, now you are here

you must come and see our little garden I was telling you so much about.'

The Waverley's house was a mansion compared to Brook Street and they were fortunate to have a substantial garden. No sooner had they stepped down the slate steps and on to the pathway that led through the middle of the lawns, Jane whispered, 'I heard you had a visit from Sir Edward Forresby?'

'Yes ... yes. He visited, but very briefly.'

Jane giggled. 'Do not fret, I forgive you! Besides, though we are at home today, Mama and I intend tomorrow to call on the Dowager Duchess of Markyate!'

Bella put her hand to her mouth to stifle a giggle. It seemed so silly to be discussing potential suitors in such a way, but she could not resist Jane's charm and ease of manner.

'Are there any other prospects, or is it just Sir Edward who has shown an interest so far?' Jane asked.

'I danced with a Mr Gray yesterday but . . . he seemed a little dull.'

'I do not think I know of a Mr Gray.'

'He is Lady Barcleywood's nephew.'

'Ah!' Jane's voice sounded dry and disapproving. 'I heard Lady Barcleywood's nephew is an attorney.'

Hot anger rose in her throat and Bella nearly tripped on an uneven paving stone. Jane touched her arm to steady her. Bella shook herself away. 'My uncle and his father are all attorneys! There is no shame in the profession!'

Jane pursed her lips. 'But have you come all this way to London to find an attorney to marry? That is the question. For if you have, then it seems a waste to me, for surely you could have picked one up in Hexham?'

Bella stared at the evergreen of the box hedging which contrasted with the brown of most of the rest of the garden. There were still only buds on the trees, no leaves. 'Jane,' she replied after some moments had passed, 'I think you are right.'

'Yes.' Jane's voice was laced with approval. 'You should set your cap a little higher than Mr Gray.'

On Bella's fourth morning in London she received her first invitation card.

Her hand trembled as she held the heavy piece of card in her hand. Miss Pamela Davenport requests the pleasure . . .

Clarissa looked up from her correspondence. They were sat in the morning room, a cool coffee-coloured room facing the front of the house. 'An invitation, my dear?'

Bella was not really listening. Her mind was fixed on the card, the first half engraved and the remainder written by hand. The Davenports lived next door!

Why, Mr Davenport might be at the moment only feet away.

'Let me see, my dear.'

Bella passed the invitation card to her aunt.

Aunt Clarissa's eyes skimmed it and shone. 'Next Monday! Oh, it will be such a crush! The Davenports are popular.' She cast her eye on to the as yet unopened pile of correspondence on the tray and found the envelope of the same size.

'And here is ours. Oh, I am pleased Miss Davenport sent an individual invitation to you. That is quite significant. It means you are regarded by the Davenport household as significantly more than an acquaintance. Poor girl, having to run the house!

'There is no Mrs Davenport. She died quite some years ago now. And the old man, quite unwell, I hear. And the eldest son, lost in the war!'

'Do we not have an engagement on Monday evening?' Bella was really not sure that she wanted to go to the Davenports'.

Aunt Clarissa frowned. 'Isabella, we must accept! It is hardly far to go!'

Where exactly on Brook Street did the Davenports live, Bella wondered. She had probably walked past the house without realising it. 'Perhaps we should have a quiet night on Tuesday?'

she suggested. 'What with the Stevensons' ball on Saturday, dinner at the Davenports' on Monday and then Lady Jane's ball next Wednesday, I shall be overcome with tiredness!'

'On Tuesday,' Aunt Clarissa replied, 'we have accepted an invitation to a recital given by the Dowager Duchess of Markyate.

'The Duke of Markyate is most eligible parti,' Aunt Clarissa said with a smile.

They made a small number of calls that afternoon, but were home in time to take an early supper. That evening they went to the opera. In their box was the Earl and Countess of Waverley and Lady Jane, and they were also joined by her brother, Henry, Viscount Thystward and his wife, Felicia.

Bella rested her gloved hands in her lap and arched her back so she was sat straight-backed and tall. It was exciting watching the stage and all the people.

It was a delightful custom, she learned, to receive visitors in one's box.

In fact, two chairs had been left empty in case anyone should join them, however briefly. And many a young gentleman came to pay his compliments to Lady Jane. But Bella discovered she herself was not without admirers.

It seemed that all of London was at the opera tonight. First came Mr Gray, Lady Barcleywood's nephew and later Sir Edward Forresby. No doubt Lady Jane would claim the latter of these visits was hers, and although Sir Edward had addressed himself to Lady Jane first, as was correct of him to do so in the order of precedence, Bella had a feeling that she was the person of prime interest.

She was even surer that she was correct in her assumptions when Sir Edward deliberately moved the empty chair he had been offered so that he was sat close next to her.

'Are you a fan of Mr Mozart, Miss Oakley?' he enquired.

'This is the first occasion I have ever visited the opera, Sir Edward, but as I find it also delightful, I suppose I must be.'

He sat with her for a good five minutes before making his excuses and leaving. He told her that he loved the way she spoke and that her turn of phrase was most refreshing.

'Am I to be a bridesmaid?' Jane whispered behind her fan.

Bella gazed down at the sea of people in the stalls, thinking on how public Sir Edward's attentions had been. Suddenly her eye was caught by the eyes of a gentleman in one of the boxes nearly opposite — Mr Davenport!

He immediately looked away.

Bella could not believe for a moment that it was really him. How could she not have noticed all this time? It was unladylike to stare, yet she endeavoured a series of quick glances. Pamela was there, looking very handsome in a hat trimmed with ostrich features.

They could not have been there before. They must have arrived late, but had he been watching her unawares? Bella fanned herself vigorously, sure her cheeks were flaming. Oh, bother the man!

'The prettiest box in London! I honour thee!'

The Duke of Markyate entered their box with a flourish and presented Lady Jane and herself each with little violet posies.

'You rascalish dandy!' growled the Earl of Waverley.

The duke bowed and left them as quickly as he had arrived.

From the whispers and exclamations Bella could hear from below, it seemed that many had witnessed Markyate's performance.

'Confounded rascal!' The earl grunted. 'Give 'em an inch and they try and flich your best claret from under your nose!'

Jane seemed to be remarkably calm, but Bella noticed that she had not managed to stop a small flush of pleasure rise up her neck and was fanning herself briskly.

The countess tapped her husband on

the sleeve. 'The Duke of Markyate is a very eligible young man.'

The next few days were less eventful and gave Bella plenty of opportunity to settle into the rounds of London life.

Two days after the opera, Sir Edward called. As she and Aunt Clarissa were at home that afternoon, the drawing room was full of ladies and clearly there was little opportunity for intimate conversation. He asked whether she had enjoyed the opera and planned to go again soon.

'I am afraid I do not know, Sir Edward.'

'Should you like to go again?'

'Oh, very much!'

'Ah, perhaps I shall arrange a box.'

Saturday, the day of the Stevensons' and her own very first ball, seemed to come around all too quickly.

She had been measured for a rather fetching confection in cream silk, with a neckline provocatively edged in plum faux roses and petite ribbons. With some apprehension she awaited its arrival from the dressmakers on Saturday morning.

The plum was a daring colour to be used for such an occasion for an unmarried girl, Aunt Clarissa advised her, but as the plum was in moderation and suited her so well, she could carry it off.

By contrast, Annabelle Stevenson, for whom the ball was being given to mark her come-out, looked insipid in her lemon yellow. It appeared not to be too much of a detraction for the men, young and old, who clamoured to dance with her.

The Stevensons' house, which they had rented, rather than purchased, was close to Brook Street, being on Grosvenor Street. It seemed hardly worth getting in the carriage and there was no time at all for Bella to try and collect her thoughts for the evening ahead before they were being ushered into the large hallway, then ante-room, and then being announced, as if into thin air of the mingling masses, by a perfectly groomed butler.

'The Honourable Charles and Mrs Cavenham. Miss Isabella Oakley.'

They passed through quickly, conscious of the queue of guests behind them. This was not York and there were too many young ladies never seen by society before for Bella to be a phenomenon, but in the plum, she was noticed.

'Miss Oakley, you say?' one observer queried.

'Cousin of the Cavenhams, I hear,' their companion replied.

Among the more critical element, there were remarks like 'Cavenhams? That will explain the plum.'

Or, 'Plum? Is she penniless?'

Or even, 'Worth twenty thousand and wearing plum? Bravo! How fashionably unnecessary!'

There could have been a thousand people in the room, but the Cavenhams appeared to know everybody. Bella smiled sweetly and tried to fix in her mind all who she met as they circled the room. It was hard work and it was a welcome respite when they came upon the Waverleys and Lady Jane.

She could relax for a moment while easy pleasantries were exchanged and she and Jane edged away slightly from the group in order to speak on things not for the ears of parents or guardians.

'I have not seen Markyate yet,' Jane whispered.

Bella felt his presence before she even saw him. She heard the clear exclamations of Pamela Davenport from a group standing just behind them and knew somehow that her brother must be with her. She heard his unmistakable cough and knew she was right.

The skin at the back of her neck prickled. He could be anything from a foot to three feet away, but he felt close enough to be standing right behind her. Her attention was drawn back to Lady Jane who was saying, 'Parliament is not sitting tonight so we may see your friend later.'

Bella blushed. In fact, the prospect of an evening without the precisely metered attentions of Sir Edward was quite refreshing, and the thought of seeing him later seemed a chore.

Lady Jane looked very animated and her eyes appeared to light up further at the approach of a young man not of Bella's acquaintance. He had fair hair which he brushed back with his hand in rather an affected manner as he rose from his bow before them.

'Lady Jane, what a pleasure to see you here.'

'Lord Caterton, may I present my cousin, Miss Isabella Oakley.'

'Ah! Miss Oakley! The name which launched a thousand ships!'

'Sir,' Jane said, 'has my cousin's name been taken in vain? Tell me, truly!'

There was a touch of amusement in Lord Caterton's eyes, which Bella found she took an instant dislike to. The man was a tease and he somehow reminded her of that dreadful Mr Montcalm.

'I will only say what I have heard,' he replied. 'A certain Miss Oakley is said to be a danger . . . to bachelors.'

He flashed his teeth as he ended on a smile and Bella did her best to appear unaffected by his comments. But in truth she had no idea what to say. Should she defend herself or say nothing, or protest? And for once, Lady Jane also seemed at a loss for words. Bella wished she were a hundred miles away from this stuffy room.

A smooth voice came from her left. 'If you would like me to remove the threat to your bachelorhood, Caterton, I should be delighted.' Mr Davenport, arrayed in severe black, gave a small bow in her direction and held out his hand. 'Miss Oakley.'

Bella took his hand and was, in moments, turning expertly at his command, safe in the protocols of the dance. She dared not look, let alone speak to him, and tried to fix her concentration on the rhythm of the music.

'Are you enjoying the season, Miss Oakley?' he said plainly as he led her into the promenade.

She was forced to look at him. To do otherwise might be noticed. He was smiling. His features were just as she remembered them.

'It is very . . . tiring,' Bella confessed. He was the gentleman who came to balls under sufferance and would rather be at Newmarket. 'Several times a day, in and out of different clothes. What I heartily dislike is the public . . . speculation. Why should it matter what precisely I wear? Whom I am seen in conversation with?'

'Or whom you dance with,' he interrupted and seemed to squeeze her hand. 'I am afraid I am in part to blame. It is common knowledge, how could it be not, since we arrived in London together. And yet, for what London has seen, we have not even spoken to one another.'

So he had not really wished to dance with her, merely advised her that they put on a show for the benefit of society.

'My sister,' he continued, 'has invited you to our crush on Monday. I assume you will come and that should scotch that piece of tittle tattle.'

Bella pushed her chin back. She could do this. She fixed her thoughts on the steps of the dance.

She wanted to say to him something that would make her more in his eyes. Not simply . . . another marriage hunting miss.

There was nothing she could say. Bella closed her eyes for a moment, enjoying the feeling of his touch as he led them to the skirl of the music. Why did this dance ever have to finish? Could it not just go on forever?

Mr Davenport drew her to one side and looked over her head about the room, wondering, she supposed, where to leave her. Bella blinked. Her lashes felt sticky. Dances could not last forever.

A young man bounded forward and asked for an introduction.

'Miss Oakley, Mr Radlett,' Mr Davenport said stiffly and left them.

As it had been in York, now Mr

Davenport had danced with her, she was not short of partners all evening. It was nearly midnight before she found herself inevitably accepting the hand of Sir Edward.

He must have sensed her tiredness, for after their dance he asked if she wished to take a rest and led her to an unoccupied chaise-longue positioned in a quiet, if there was such a thing, corner.

She did feel tired, having sat down only briefly once the whole evening and she had perhaps drunk a little more than was wise. She took a seat gratefully and allowed Sir Edward to talk about summers spent on the river at Oxford without interruption.

'You will have never enjoyed a summer's day by the Cherwell,' he said, and before she could answer, 'I would be honoured, Miss Oakley, if you would grant me your hand in marriage?'

Bella found herself suddenly wide-awake. 'Sir Edward . . . ' She did not know what to say.

9

Bella swallowed. He was looking at her intently and she wished there was a foot more air between them.

Sir Edward was a rising star in government. Who was to say that his baronetcy would not be succeeded by some greater honour? She had been made a very good offer.

'I realise that this has come as a sudden surprise to you, Miss Oakley.' He leaned closer and Bella's heart quickened. 'I do not wish to press you for an answer now. I am content to wait for a few days.'

She wondered if he would want to kiss her hand, but he did not. They were of course still in the ballroom where anyone might see.

Bella nodded as he rose to leave her. She had no words. Matters would be clearer in the crisp daylight of tomorrow.

Sunday was a quiet day. The events of the night before kept threatening to crowd her mind but at church she concentrated on the hymns and the sermon and once home again, on her correspondence.

All day two gentlemen kept intruding into her thoughts. They were of course Mr Davenport and Sir Edward. She had been tempted to mention something to Aunt Clarissa, but there had not been an opportune moment.

Yes. She felt obliged to seek her guidance, yet something was keeping her back. What if her aunt was forceful in the direction of Sir Edward? It was better to leave things alone for now.

Lady Jane appeared the following afternoon to collect her for a drive in Hyde Park. Bella quickly pulled on her gloves and Spencer jacket and came downstairs to find Jane standing in the hall waving a newspaper. 'Bella! Have you not seen this?'

Jane thrust into her hands a copy of

yesterday's Morning Post and pointed her at the right page. 'Look, there is a report of the Stevenson's ball.'

'I was so busy yesterday,' Bella began.

'Listen!' Jane read aloud from the paper. 'Miss Stevenson wore pale yellow but did not fare badly despite this ill advised colour.'

'Oh, how cruel!' Bella's hand flew to her mouth.

'But we would wager more hearts will be broken,' continued Jane, 'by the young lady who sported a daring plum neckline.'

Bella kept her hand clasped over her mouth and muffled a squeak. Had she heard correctly?

'Congratulations! You have made it! Everyone will want to know you now. All you have to do now is wait for them to hammer down the door! Now are you ready, for Mama is waiting outside in the carriage?'

Bella thrust her hands by her sides and stood tall. 'Surely some other ladies were wearing plum?'

Jane shook her head. 'Of course it's you!'

'Are you not mentioned, Jane?'

'No, but if you are seen in our carriage I hope to benefit from the association. Bella, please smile, it's only a newspaper!'

'I am not certain I wish to be in a newspaper . . . as a breaker of gentlemen's hearts.'

'It's only tittle tattle! All it means is that you have more admirers than you think. Not only Sir Edward.'

Bella felt her cheeks colour. If only she did, and if only his name was Mr Davenport. They stepped outside and the breeze was cooling.

Bella sat back in the Waverley's carriage and smiled. It was a pleasantly warm day and she was glad she had chosen to wear the orange blossom muslin and matching parasol. There was some pale sunshine, hardly enough to warrant the parasol, but there were other ladies taking no chances with their complexions.

Aunt Clarissa and the Countess of Waverley accompanied them and looked resplendent in their matronly colours, but all the attention was on her and Lady Jane who wore a very pale violet blue.

It seemed as if all of London was riding round Hyde Park, just watching everyone else.

'Look!' whispered Jane suddenly. 'See over there? That rather grand phaeton.'

Bella threw back a quick glance. It was the Duke of Markyate! And at his side was a very attractive lady. What was Jane feeling?

'Mama, who is that lady with the Duke of Markyate?' Jane said.

The Countess replied, 'Jane, your gloves are not clean, why did you not change them before we came out?'

'Oh, then the lady is not someone who is in Society?'

'Look,' said the Countess, 'here comes Mr Fitzgerald. Smile, Jane.'

Jane smiled and nodded at the gentleman passing on horseback and he lifted his hat in return.

'Surely I can do better than marry an Irishman, Mama?' she said after he had gone.

'You would do best not to throw away anything at this early stage of the Season. We have not even had your ball yet.'

'But Isabella has not even been in London as long as I and she has already had an offer!'

Bella dropped her parasol and the breeze whipped it out of the carriage before anyone could catch it.

'Bella! An offer? Is this true?' asked Aunt Clarissa.

'Stop!' said the Countess to the driver. He looked around helplessly as he could not leave hold of the ribbons in order to jump down from the coach and catch the wayward parasol.

'I will go,' Bella began to move.

'Certainly not!' snapped the Countess. She laid her gloved hands across Bella's.

'Excuse me,' a familiar male voice

said. 'Might we be of assistance?'

Mr Davenport mounted on a fine chestnut stallion drew up beside them. Just behind him was Mr Paxton-Claremont on a very tall bay. The Countess's furrowed brows disappeared as she smiled.

'Mr Davenport! Mr Paxton-Claremont! How fortuitous! Miss Oakley has lost her parasol in a vicious gust of wind.' The Countess waved her hand to the left in the direction of the parasol which lay caught at the base of an oak tree.

The corners of Mr Davenport's lips quirked.

First my straw bonnet, now my parasol, Bella thought. It was no wonder he found it amusing.

There was nothing she could do but be thankful the day was cool despite the sun and concentrate on keeping the heat out of her cheeks as she watched Mr Davenport slide down from his mount while Mr Paxton-Claremont held the reins.

He picked up the parasol and strode

over the grass so that he stood right beside her, his face looking up to hers as he handed Bella the parasol.

'Unbroken,' he said, and very low added, 'this time.'

'Thank you, Mr Davenport,' Bella replied loudly. She did not want to share a private joke with him here in public. 'And thank you, Mr Paxton-Claremont.'

'Thank you,' Aunt Clarissa said. 'You must — '

'Thank you, gentlemen,' the Countess interrupted. 'Drive on.'

The driver flicked the ribbons and they moved away.

'What a spectacle!' the Countess muttered. 'We were very lucky to have been in a quiet part of the park.'

'Yes, lucky indeed.' Aunt Clarissa smiled. 'Mr Davenport is a delightful gentleman.'

Oh dear, Bella thought, sure now that her cheeks were red. 'My offer was not from Mr Davenport.'

'Oh, was it not?' Aunt Clarissa's eyes

widened with surprise.

'It was from Sir Edward Forresby. He proposed at the Stevenson's ball, but I do not think he has approached Charles yet.'

'How underhand!' the Countess snapped. 'He should have approached Charles first.'

'But what was your answer? Did you refuse him?'

'Sir Edward is waiting for my answer.'

'Oh dear, this is most awkward.' Aunt Clarissa rearranged her skirts. 'For Charles was approached this morning by a gentleman who asked for permission to address you. And Charles gave that permission unaware of Sir Edward's interest.'

'Good afternoon!' the Countess shouted at the carriage passing them. Its occupants nodded.

'We shall have to talk about this when we get home,' Aunt Clarissa said.

'Sorry, Bella,' Jane said. 'I did not mean to get you into trouble.'

Who had asked for permission to address her? Bella wondered. It must be Mr Davenport. She could think of no-one else.

'Sir Edward is universally acknowledged to be a most honourable gentleman,' Aunt Clarissa said later. They were shut in the morning room.

Bella stared at the floor.

'He is clever and kind,' continued Aunt Clarissa. 'He does not gamble or drink to any serous degree. All in all, Charles and I consider that you should accept Sir Edward's proposal.'

'But . . . what about the other gentleman?' — Bella could not stop herself saying.

'The other gentleman, whilst still eligible in his own right, I am sure, would not have as much to recommend him as Sir Edward. You have been very fortunate to secure Sir Edward's affections and so quickly. It is not to be tossed aside by a whim.'

Aunt Clarissa stood up and left the room shutting the door firmly behind her.

Bella stared into the fire until it blurred. She pulled her handkerchief out of her ridicule and dabbed her eyes.

It was like the worst kind of nightmare — one that she could make no sense of. There could be no reasonable objection to Sir Edward's offer. He was as Aunt Clarissa described — a man of honour and ability.

And yet, there was nothing in his step that made her tremble. His presence did not make her blind to all that was going on around her. These were all things that happened when Mr Davenport was there. But Mr Davenport had not made an offer, whereas Sir Edward Forresby awaited her answer.

Bella walked over to the window which looked out on Brook Street. The match had so many advantages and she must think on these and not allow her mind to wander into the clouds.

Carriages and carts clattered through the street outside. London was busy as usual.

Then she saw him. In the corner of

her eye she had been aware the man had been loitering on the opposite side of the street all the while.

He had been reading a pamphlet and now he lowered it and stared directly at their house. It was Mr Montcalm!

Bella threw herself back behind the curtain crushing the velvet in her fingers. Her heart pounded. What was Mr Montcalm doing here? Watching the house?

How long had he been there? She did not know if he had been waiting since they had come home in the carriage.

Bella peered slowly around the curtain. He was still there. He bent down to tie his shoelaces and then struck up a conversation with a waiting jarvey.

He showed no signs of leaving Brook Street. And every so often he glanced up at their house.

Bella pulled herself away from the window and found Charles in the library.

'What if there was a burglar outside?

What could be done about it?'

Charles looked up from his newspaper. 'Isabella, you look rather unwell. What's the matter?'

'If there was a man lurking outside, a burglar, what could be done?'

'Well . . . ' Charles folded his newspaper and placed it down on the bureaux. 'We could send for the Bow Street Runners.'

'There is a man loitering outside,' Bella explained.

'I would think it likely one of those scoundrel newspaper reporters. Can't see a burglar standing around in the daylight for all to see. Is he watching our house?'

'Yes, he appears to be.' Should she tell Charles she knew who the man was? Of one thing she was sure — Mr Montcalm was not a newspaper man.

'He probably wants to see what you are wearing to the Davenport's tonight,' Charles said.

Bella had chosen, with Clarissa's advice, an apple green Indian silk gown trimmed with moss green velvet. There was a matching pelisse in the moss, which of course she would remove on arrival but she felt like a very smart lady about town.

The Davenport's house was modest in comparison to the pile belonging to the Earl of Waverley, but as grand as the Cavenham's if not perhaps quite as large.

But the crush of carriages outside, and bodies inside boded for a large party. Bella found herself strangely glad as they came into the large drawing-room full of people she did not recognise. She could hide among all the people. Maybe she would not see Mr Davenport all evening?

Her chest tightened at that thought. After all, she had taken so much care over her toilette. And . . . she wanted to ask him about Mr Montcalm.

'Miss Oakley, we meet again.' Lord Caterton lifted her fingers and kissed them.

'Lord Caterton.' Bella dipped her

head in a nod. Aunt Clarissa and Uncle Charles seemed to be busy in conversation with the couple next to them.

'Will you make tomorrow's Morning Post, Miss Plum, I am sorry, Miss Oakley?' Lord Caterton said. 'That is the question on everyone's lips.'

'I should imagine there are greater speculations.' Bella replied and tried to keep the pique from her voice.

'Such as, will the government win in the house tonight,' he replied.

Did everyone in London know of Sir Edward's offer? Bella took a hasty sip of champagne. 'What fine weather we are having, Lord Caterton. Tell me, is it usual for London at this time of year?'

Bella thrust her chin in the air. She was caught in the coal-black gaze of Mr Davenport standing right in front of her.

'Caterton, would you excuse me if I stole Miss Oakley for a moment.' Mr Davenport held out his arm. He looked immaculate, dressed from head to foot in black save his white shirt and cravat.

Bella flicked open her fan and fanned herself vigorously.

'It is quite improper for me to invite you away like this,' Mr Davenport said as he led her out of the drawing-room and through the hall towards the back of the house. 'But it might be impossible later if the crush becomes unbearable. And I wanted to talk to you.'

He opened a door. 'The library. The party has not yet expanded into here.'

A low fire burned in the small grate. Otherwise the room was unlit. Mr Davenport picked up a taper which stood on a cabinet outside.

In the dark silence Bella could hear herself breathing. Mr Davenport stepped forward, his tread making a floorboard creak, and held his taper up high.

Bella looked above the mahogany panelling and to the pictures. They were all of horses except for one.

It was a small head and shoulders portrait of a young woman in an old fashioned gown, her neck swathed in ruffles of lace and her hair unnaturally white with powder.

Yet the resemblance was unmistakable.

'The portrait,' Mr Davenport said in a low voice, 'is of our mother.'

'Yes, I had noticed the resemblance,' she said.

'And the handsome black stallion you see here?' He waved the taper at the next painting. 'That was Forge, my father's favourite hunter.'

'Your father — '

'Does not hunt any more, no, nor is even able to come up to town to see Forge's portrait, or his late wife's.'

The backs of Bella's eyes felt a little hot, as if tears threatened. She did not know Mr Davenport's father and yet she felt sorry for him as an invalid.

It was not only the father. She also felt sorry for Mr Davenport. A log fell in the grate causing sparks and she saw his face quite clearly. His expression was fixed, but beneath it something was bothering him. He waved the taper at the shelves. 'Have you read Mrs Ratcliffe?'

And they were quite alone in this room. Not even the servants could know they were here or someone would have rushed in to light the room for them.

He could not have wanted to speak to her about Mrs Ratcliffe! Bella took a long breath. 'Mr Davenport, while there is the opportunity I wanted to say something to you.'

'Oh.'

She forced herself to look at him. His eyes returned her regard carefully. The flame of the taper flickered but his eyes did not. They were steady. For one moment she had the notion that he might kiss her.

He broke her gaze and the moment was lost.

Bella swallowed. 'Mr . . . Mr Mont-calm was standing outside on Brook Street this afternoon. W-watching our house.'

Something like alarm crossed Mr Davenport's eyes. 'Are you sure?'

'I am sure.'

'Miss Oakley.' His voice sounded very stiff and he looked as though his thoughts were elsewhere. 'Let us return to the drawing-room.'

What had she done!

Bella did not allow herself to reflect on what had happened until much later when she was alone. She sat at her dressing table staring into its mirror as the maid brushed her hair ready for bed.

How had it come about that she had imagined he wanted to kiss her?

She could not answer that question. Either he had wanted to kiss her or she had imagined it. If she had imagined it, she was foolish indeed to start building castles in the air.

Tomorrow it was likely that Sir Edward might come for his answer. He was an honourable man and the right thing to do would be to accept his suit.

If Mr Davenport had thought to offer for her, it seemed his will was not strong enough to pursue it after she had told him about Mr Montcalm whose activities it seem to be far more pressing to attend to.

Bella sat bolt upright in bed. What if Mr Montcalm had not been watching her house at all, but the Davenport's. Was Pamela Davenport in danger.

10

The following day was uneventful. They were at home in the afternoon, but no gentleman of any significance called. In the evening they attended the Dowager Duchess of Markyate's musicale and Bella was curious to see if the dashing Duke would be there. He was not, much to his mother's annoyance. Nor were the Davenports or Sir Edward.

It was as if time was ticking past slowly, and yet nothing was happening. And Mr Montcalm was not in the street outside.

Wednesday had always promised to be exciting because it was the day of the ball, Bella considered as she washed her hands and face using the pretty basin and ewer in her dressing-room that morning.

Once dressed she forced herself to go downstairs for breakfast. She was alone in the dining-room for only about five minutes until Charles came in carrying that abomination of all newspapers, The Morning Post.

'Do not fret, you have escaped today's edition,' he said, dropping the paper on to the table and coming over to join her at the buffet.

Bella forked a small slice of ham on to her plate and sat down.

She found she was not hungry. She scraped some butter on to a slice of toast and watched Charles tuck into his eggs.

'Good morning!' Aunt Clarissa swept in and immediately helped herself from the coffee pot.

Charles looked up suddenly from his plate. 'Ah, Isabella. I forgot to mention this to you yesterday, but Mr Davenport asked if he might call at eleven o'clock.'

Aunt Clarissa put her coffee cup down with a clatter. 'My dear child, are you ready to receive him? Sir Edward has not called has he? Perhaps . . . ' She did not finish what she was saying.

Bella glanced up at the clock which said it was ten minutes to ten. 'Yes.'

'That clock stopped yesterday,' Charles said, pulling out his pocket watch. 'It's very nearly eleven now.'

'Oh!' Bella jumped to her feet.

At the same moment there was a knock and the door opened. Bromham, the butler, came in and said, 'Mr Davenport is here to see Miss Oakley.'

Bella sat down again with a thud. Her hands felt damp. She wiped them with her napkin.

'Please show Mr Davenport into the drawing-room and say that Miss Oakley will attend him shortly,' Charles said.

Bromham nodded and closed the door behind him.

'I should wait five minutes, my dear, before you go and see him.' Clarissa said. 'You do wish to receive him alone, do you not? Or is there anything you would like Charles and I to do?'

Bella glanced at the clock which still said ten minutes to ten. 'No. No, thank you. I will see Mr Davenport alone.'

A sharp rap on the door and Brom-ham returned. 'Excuse me, but there is another visitor. Sir Edward Forresby has just arrived to see Miss Oakley — '

'Oh!' Clarissa exclaimed. 'Charles . . . ?'

Bella felt as if she'd turned to ice. Both here. At the same time. How . . . ?

'Show Sir Edward into the library, Bromham,' Charles's voice rang out clearly. 'And inform him that Miss Oakley will see him shortly.'

Bromham bowed and left them.

'Now, my dear,' Clarissa said, rising and coming over to stand beside her. 'You must see Mr Davenport quickly and then you may attend to Sir Edward at leisure.'

Bella rose and found that her legs would barely carry her.

Aunt Clarissa patted her lightly on the arm. 'Good luck,' she whispered.

Bella took a deep breath and pushed her shoulders back, and walked out of the dining-room and into the hall.

Mr Davenport was coming down the

stairs — two at a time. He saw her and slowed his pace. He paused on the half-landing. He nodded. 'Good morning, Miss Oakley.'

'Mr Davenport . . . ' Bella gripped her skirt in order to begin climbing the stairs. 'Our drawing-room is on the first floor.'

She was too late. He hurried down the remaining stairs until he stood next to her. 'I bid you farewell,' he said, pulling at his cravat. 'Until this evening. And congratulations.'

'Congratulations?'

'On your happy circumstance. Sir Edward informed me of your news.'

'Pardon? Wait — '

He strode past her, helping himself to his coat and gloves from the stand before the footman who came running from the back of the hallway and could not even reach him.

'Mr Davenport!' Bella could feel tears pricking at the back of her head. What had Sir Edward told him? 'Wait! There has been a mistake!'

'Good day,' he said with force.

The footman jumped to open the front door. His dark coat swirled as he departed. She heard his footsteps clattering down the stone steps outside.

It was inconceivable that she could chase after him into Brook Street. Bella swallowed as the footman carefully shut the front door.

What had Sir Edward said? And how dare he?

Bella picked up her skirts and mounted the stairs. She was hot with an unexplainable hurt, but it was slowly being taken over by fury.

Sir Edward was not in the library as he should have been, but in the drawing-room. He stood with his back to the fire and smiled as she entered the room. 'My dear Isabella — '

'Did you . . . did you tell him that we were betrothed?'

Sir Edward looked taken aback. 'Naturally, my dear, he — '

'You had no right to do so.' Bella stood up as tall as she could.

'My dear, you appear a trifle vexed.' He stepped forward. 'But you do not seem to realise why Mr Davenport called to see you this morning.'

'Why did he call?' Bella held her hands fast together. She must remain calm.

'He would offer you his hand, my dear. It appeared he had no notion you were already spoken for.'

Bella stepped back and hit the arm of a chaise. She reached out and held the arm to steady herself.

'Do not worry, Mr Davenport is a gentleman and will not breathe a word of our engagement before the official announcement is made. You have nothing to fear — '

'We are not engaged. Nor ever shall be.'

Sir Edward's eyes clouded. 'You cannot — '

'I am afraid I cannot marry where there is no affection.' Bella ran to the door. 'Good day, Sir Edward.'

She didn't stop until she reached the cool of the morning-room where she sat very still and did not let herself weep.

There was a gentle tap on the door and Aunt Clarissa came into the morning-room followed by a maid carrying a tea tray.

'Is he . . . is he gone?'

'Sir Edward left directly after your interview,' Aunt Clarissa replied. She came over to sit next to Bella.

Bella dabbed her eyes with her handkerchief and blew her nose.

'It would appear that this morning has been unsatisfactory,' Aunt Clarissa remarked. 'Would you like some tea?'

'I told Sir Edward I could not marry him,' Bella said. She explained how Sir Edward had informed Mr Davenport that they were betrothed.

'I must ask you one question,' Aunt Clarissa said putting the teapot down now she had finished with it. 'Do you desire to marry either gentleman?'

Bella bit her lip. 'I had hoped . . . that Mr Davenport had come here this morning to make me an offer. I would have accepted that offer.'

'It was Mr Davenport who asked for permission to address you. But now that there has been this misunderstanding we must think what to do.'

Bella sipped her hot tea.

Aunt Clarissa looked thoughtful before saying, 'We should clear this up with haste today. You must send him a note.'

'A note?'

'I should not normally encourage an unmarried girl to commence a private correspondence with a gentleman, but in the circumstances we must correct Mr Davenport's misapprehension. You shall ask him very simply to call again and all will be well.'

Clarissa rose and went over to the escritoire. 'The subject matter is rather delicate so we shall make no mention of that. And you will simply sign with your initials not your full name.'

Bella sat down at the escritoire. After several attempts the missal was at last complete.

My dear A. D.,

I am sorry we missed the opportunity of speaking this morning. If it is not inconvenient I shall be at home if you would call again today. I have certain facts I would like to furnish you with by way of explanation.

Your servant, E. O.

They waited for the reply or the gentleman himself. Bella found herself constantly glancing at the pretty ormolu clock on the mantelpiece. She had no needlework or correspondence to apply herself to and so was trying with little success to read a book.

It was a travel journal and had looked interesting but the detail and novelty was too overwhelming for her to get into. She kept having to turn back a page to remind herself where she had got to and every time she did this she also could not help looking again at the clock.

A quarter to two.

Two o'clock.

The boy must have reached the

Davenport's by now. Perhaps he had her note in his hands already?

A quarter past two. No reply yet.

Half past two. Bella put the volume down and went to the window which faced the front to see if she could see anyone coming. There was nothing except the usual traffic and reassuring patter of horses' hooves and rattle of carriages.

Bella sat down again. Should she change her book? She was just about to get up again and go to the library to do this when there was a knock on the door.

The reply was here. Bella seized at the letter offered elegantly on a silver tray by Bromham, her hands trembling. She tore at the seal, opened it and read.

My dear E. O.,
    Thank you kindly for your note. No explanation is required.
    A. D.

She passed it to Aunt Clarissa.

'Oh, the stupid man!' Clarissa said

173

and threw it down on the escritoire. 'If you truly want to marry him, you will have to speak to him at the Waverley's this evening. There is nothing else for it!'

It was eerie standing in the double-height ceiling ballroom as they waited for the first guests to arrive. They had dined at the Waverley's and the handful of dinner guests now sipped champagne in near silence.

Her dress was delightful — cream coloured and decorated with a green classically-inspired motif and small bud silk roses — and even the Earl of Waverley had complemented her. But her hands were damp inside her silk gloves, and trembling as she held her glass of champagne.

The orchestra were assembled although the dancing would not start until later. Bows drawn across strings scratched and hummed as they tuned their instruments.

The sound of footsteps and chatter. The two wigged footmen at the double doors to the ballroom stood to attention and the Waverley's butler stepped into action.

The first guests were arriving. Bella fanned herself quickly before letting her fan dangle from her wrist ready to greet them.

At ten o'clock the Duke of Markyate claimed Jane for the first dance. Bella found she was happy for Jane, and yet . . .

Mr Davenport had not arrived.

She danced with Lord Caterton and then with Mr Paxton-Claremont and her third dance was with an officer in the dragoons by the name of Captain Berrystead.

'Would you like a glass of champagne?' the captain said, drawing her to one side as the dance ended. 'Or ratafia?'

'Champagne, please. That would be very kind.' Bella watched the other couples disperse while the captain fetched her champagne.

And then she saw him. His lean hand raked through his hair in an uncharacteristically nervous gesture. Beneath him, or so it seemed for he was so tall, stood Miss Paxton-Claremont. She fluttered her eyelashes and giggled at something Mr Davenport said.

'Miss Oakley?'

Captain Berrystead had reappeared and handed her a glass of champagne. It was an effort not to drop it.

She held the glass firmly and took a sip, no, a gulp and nearly choked. Bella coughed and spluttered.

'Good heavens! Are you all right?' He patted her on the shoulder.

'Y-yes.' Bella tried to catch her breath but some of the champagne had gone down the wrong way and it was difficult. She coughed again.

Out of the corner of her eye she saw Miss Paxton-Claremont tilt back her head and laugh. And Mr Davenport smiled at her.

Bella shut her eyes for the moment and coughed some more.

'You had better sit down for a while. Get your breath back.' The captain steered her through the crowds.

'Yes, I'll be all right in a few moments,' Bella managed. 'Thank you.'

She left the ballroom and ignored the footman who slanted his hand in the direction of the ladies powder room. She wanted to be alone.

She followed the corridor until it came into the main hall. Off here, at the front of the house and on the ground floor was the library. The Waverleys would not mind if she rested for a few moments.

There was a fire lit and in front of it two large wing-backed chairs. Bella sunk into one of them and curled up with her feet tucked beneath her. She could stay here undisturbed. Any servant popping their head around the door would not be able to see her only the high back of the chair.

The fire was warm on her face and bare shoulders but wet tears slid down her cheeks. It was too late. Now that Mr Davenport believed her engaged he had transferred his affections to Miss Paxton-Claremont.

The door to the library opened with a creak. Bella gulped back tears and froze as two pairs of footsteps came into the room. The door was shut.

A woman's voice said, 'now you'd better be quick for you should not be here at all.'

Pamela Davenport!

Bella hardly dared breathe. She must be in the middle of some assignation. At the very least some private conversation Bella had no right to overhear. She had better get up now and leave the room, before —

'I can be very brief. Everything is arranged,' said Mr Montcalm.

Mr Montcalm was here. Bella could not move. A piece of coal on the fire hissed.

The door to the library was pushed open with violence. 'Montcalm!' shouted Mr Davenport. 'You have no — '

Bella threw herself out of her chair as another gentleman entered the room — the Duke of Markyate.

'Miss Oakley!' Pamela's hand shot to her mouth.

Everyone looked at her. The Duke of Markyate pulled a pistol from under his coat and pointed it at Mr Davenport. He said in a slow drawl. 'This is all going to be very simple. Davenport, your sister is marrying me.'

'Stop!' Bella shouted and ran forward. 'You can't force Pamela to do anything!'

Mr Montcalm threw his head back and laughed. 'Miss Oakley, you have misread the situation, I assure you.'

'Indeed,' Pamela added and smiled. 'Darling, put the pistol away. Anthony has agreed to give his permission!' She skipped over to the tall, arrogant looking man. He tucked his pistol away and then lifted her hand to his mouth and kissed it. With tenderness.

Bella looked at them both and at Mr Davenport whose expression was fixed and unemotional. 'I'm sorry,' she muttered and made for the door.

'Not so fast.' Mr Davenport moved so that he blocked her path to the door.

Bella blinked. The room was wobbling.

'Miss Oakley!' Mr Davenport was at her elbow. 'All is well.' He turned to the others. 'Will you leave us alone, please.'

'Yes, yes,' Mr Montcalm replied. 'As your wife to be — '

'Pardon?' Bella pulled herself upright. And who was going to be whose wife?

'You will marry me, won't you?' Mr Davenport's voice was very soft, and she could feel the tingle of his breath on her cheek as he leaned in close to her ear.

The carriage clock on the mantelpiece chimed the hour. 'Please say you will, Isabella.' Pamela's eyes were opened wide. 'Anthony thinks so very highly of you.'

'Of course you will,' Mr Davenport said, his chin high in the air.

'But — '

'But who else would have sent that note this afternoon?' He lowered his voice. 'You seemed so anxious to inform me that you were not engaged to Sir Edward?'

Bella looked up into his eyes and saw

they were dancing. 'Yes. Yes, I will marry you.'

'Well, thank heavens for that.' The Duke of Markyate moved towards the door. 'Shall we get some champagne?'

'No.' Mr Davenport's voice was as hard as iron.

'Let us go,' Pamela said.

The Duke and Mr Montcalm followed her out of the room.

'I should explain to you what has been going on.' Mr Davenport lifted her hands to his lips. Her spine trembled.

'Was . . . was Pamela considering . . . running away with the Duke of Markyate,' Bella said swiftly. There was something she must get off her chest.

Mr Davenport's eyes lingered on her. 'Yes. And Mr Montcalm is his oldest crony and was aiding the whole scheme. I stopped them . . . last night.'

'I . . . I discovered Pamela had left her room that night at the inn when you chased after that pistol shot.'

His eyebrows raised. 'You said nothing — '

'Pamela asked me not to.' Bella felt ashamed.

Mr Davenport sighed. 'The man is a rake and a scoundrel, but Pamela assures me she loves him, and he her in return.' His eyes twinkled. 'And when I discovered for myself how powerful an emotion love can be, I had to relent and allow the match.'

He still grasped her hands tight in his and now drew her even closer to him so that her chest brushed against his coat. 'Do you think I did the right thing?'

Bella found herself unable to answer him.

His countenance closed the distance between itself and hers, and the scent of his cologne tickled her nostrils.

She forgot all about sneezing as his lips touched hers.

We do hope that you have enjoyed reading this large print book.

Did you know that all of our titles are available for purchase?

We publish a wide range of high quality large print books including:
Romances, Mysteries, Classics
General Fiction
Non Fiction and Westerns

Special interest titles available in large print are:
The Little Oxford Dictionary
Music Book, Song Book
Hymn Book, Service Book

Also available from us courtesy of Oxford University Press:
Young Readers' Dictionary
(large print edition)
Young Readers' Thesaurus
(large print edition)

For further information or a free brochure, please contact us at:
Ulverscroft Large Print Books Ltd.,
The Green, Bradgate Road, Anstey,
Leicester, LE7 7FU, England.
Tel: (00 44) **0116 236 4325**
Fax: (00 44) **0116 234 0205**

RELUCTANT DESIRE

Kay Gregory

Laura was furious. It was bad enough having to share her home with a stranger for a month — but being forced to live under the same roof as the notorious Adam Veryan . . . His midnight-dark eyes challenged Laura to forget about her fiancé Rodney, and she knew instinctively that Adam would be a dangerous, disruptive presence in her life. She'd be a fool to surrender her heart to such careless custody . . . but could she resist Adam's flirtatious charm?

CHANCE ENCOUNTER

Shirley Heaton

When her fiancé cancels their forthcoming wedding, Sophie books a holiday in Spain to overcome her disappointment. After wrongly accusing a stranger, Matt, of taking her suitcase at the airport, she is embarrassed to find he is staying at her hotel. When she discovers a mysterious package inside her suitcase, she suspects that the package is linked to him. But then she finds herself falling in love with Matt — and, after a series of mysterious encounters, she is filled with doubts . . .